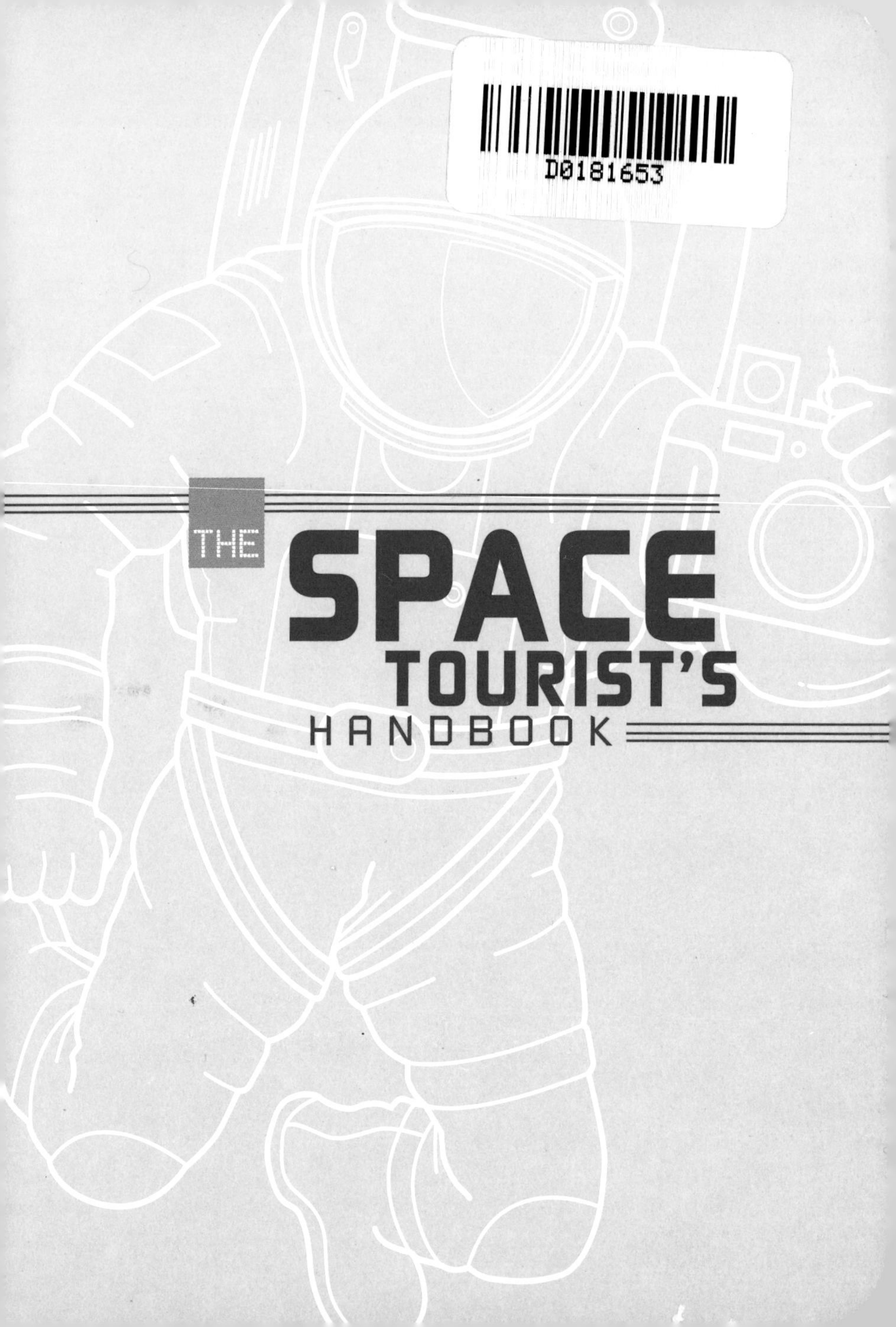
THE
SPACE
TOURIST'S
HANDBOOK

ACKNOWLEDGMENTS

Eric Anderson thanks James Oberg, Emily Anderson, Richard Jennings, and the entire Space Adventures team, especially Marsel Gubaydullin, Inessa Heeger, and Chris Faranetta. Josh "Buzz" Piven thanks his co-author Eric Anderson and all the space cadets at Quirk Books: To infinity . . . and beyond!

Library of Congress Cataloging in Publication Number: 2005922081

ISBN: 1-59474-066-6

Printed in Singapore

Typeset in Russell Square

Designed by Bryn Ashburn

Illustrations by Stuart Holmes

All photos courtesy of Space Adventures except images on pages 18, 19, and 23, which are provided courtesy of NASA.

Distributed in North America by Chronicle Books
85 Second Street
San Francisco, CA 94105

---

10 9 8 7 6 5 4 3 2 1

Quirk Books
215 Church Street
Philadelphia, PA 19106
www.quirkbooks.com

THE SPACE TOURIST'S HANDBOOK

WHERE TO GO, WHAT TO SEE, AND HOW TO PREPARE FOR THE RIDE OF YOUR LIFE

BY ERIC ANDERSON,
PRESIDENT OF
SPACE adventures

and JOSHUA PIVEN, co-author of
The Worst-Case Scenario Survival Handbook

CONTENTS

This book is dedicated to astronauts past and present—the brave men and women who have paved the way for space tourists of tomorrow.

FOREWORD BY DENNIS TITO

On April 28, 2001, I climbed aboard a Soyuz rocket that blasted into the heavens, beginning an eight-day round trip excursion to the International Space Station. On that day, I became the 415th person to enter space—and the first person to pay to travel in space.

I have been interested in space travel since I was a teenager and the first Sputnik was launched. With the hope of becoming an astronaut, I earned degrees in aeronautical and aerospace engineering. But instead of flying in space myself, I spent five years in the early 1960s working at the Jet Propulsion Laboratory to develop trajectories for Mariner Mars and Venus probes. Eventually, I shifted career paths and entered the world of finance. I helped to found an investment technology firm, Wilshire Associates Incorporated, which during the last three decades we've built into a leading global investment technology, investment consulting, and investment management firm.

Even with all of my business and financial success, I never lost my fascination with space.

In June 2000, after intensive negotiations, it was announced that I would travel to the Russian Space Station, Mir. However, with months of training completed, I learned Mir would be taken out of orbit and sent crashing into the ocean. Not one to let a goal out of my grasp, I turned to Eric Anderson, the co-author of this book—and the CEO of a company called Space Adventures. Eric believed that space tourism was the perfect way to bring much-needed development funds to space programs around the world. Like me, Eric had followed the planning and construction of the International Space Station with great interest. We knew the Russian space program conducted routine eight-day "taxi" missions to the International Space Station to rotate staff and deliver new supplies. Only two cosmonauts are required for these missions—but the Soyuz rocket has three seats.

Eric worked with me and the Russian space program to reserve the empty third seat on the Soyuz rocket on a flight set for late April 2001. My trip would involve a five-day stay at the International Space Station, with the cost covering the salaries of more than ten thousand Russian space workers for at least a year.

Believe me, writing the check was the easiest part. I trained for six months—more than 900 hours—in Russia's Yuri Gagarin Cosmonauts Training Center in Star City, just outside Moscow. I took courses on spacecraft systems and how to fix them. I studied the Russian sections of the Space Station and learned how to deal with emergencies. I spent countless hours in the gym and running on the grounds of Star City, strengthening and toning my 60-year-old body so I would be ready for the physical exertion of space.

And if you're serious about space travel, you'll need to be prepared to do all of these things, too. Space tourism is a lot of hard work. No one is going to babysit you, no matter how much money you spend.

But the results are worth it. After the births of my children, visiting the International Space Station was the most wonderful experience of my life. My physical and emotional reactions went far beyond what I expected. And in my own small way, I have opened the door to other would-be space tourists. For certainly there are thousands—maybe millions—who would love to journey beyond the earth.

I wish you much luck and success in your own space travels—and wherever else life takes you. With goals set and a solid work ethic, there is no limit to where you can go.

Bon voyage!

Dennis A. Tito

INTRODUCTION

A trip to outer space is like no vacation you've ever experienced—complete with breathtaking scenery, edge-of-your-seat adventure, billion-dollar technology, and memories to last a lifetime.

And now such a trip is available to the general public. As an astronaut, you can be among the first humans to travel beyond planet Earth—and you don't have to train with NASA to get there. The space tourism industry—once the province of science fiction writers—is now a full-fledged reality, and business is booming.

But before you don your spacesuit and blast off, it's worth taking a moment to learn about the astronauts and cosmonauts who came before you. Today's space vacation is truly a trip perched on the shoulders of giants; without the extreme skill and courage of these pioneers, space tourism would not be possible.

A HISTORY OF SPACE TRAVEL

On April 12, 1961, a young Soviet Air Force pilot named Yuri Gagarin left planet Earth behind in a spaceship called *Vostok 1* and became the first human being to fly in space. Gagarin orbited the Earth a single time and returned safely to the desert floor of Kazakhstan two hours later. The era of space travel was born, and the first race in the greatest technological competition of the twentieth century—a race between two superpowers with competing visions for the future of mankind—was history. The Soviets had won.

But the contest was far from over.

Three weeks later—in Cape Canaveral, Florida—American Navy pilot Alan Shepard blasted into space on a sub-orbital Mercury Redstone rocket. The charismatic young astronaut ignited the passion of the American people and set the stage for the decade to come, a decade of spectacular successes and crushing defeats, a time of imagination and wonderment at the promises and possibilities of space travel.

And what a time it was. The 1960s saw many heroes explore the "final frontier" for the United States, for the Soviet Union, and, most importantly, for the world. The first woman in space, Valentina Tereshkova, orbited the Earth in 1963. A Russian cosmonaut completed the first spacewalk in 1965. The first space station, Salyut 1, was conceived in 1969 and sent into orbit two years later. And the earliest astronauts and cosmonauts from both

>> FROM MISSION CONTROL

We've all heard recordings of Neil Armstrong saying, "That's one small step for man, one giant leap for mankind." But when Armstrong returned to Earth, he discovered that a very small word had been garbled during the transmission. He claims to have said, "That's one small step for a man, one giant leap for mankind." Nevertheless, it's the abridged version that you'll find in *Bartlett's Quotations*.

countries lost their lives in the pursuit of space exploration.

The climactic moment of the decade occurred on July 20, 1969, when two young Americans named Neil Armstrong and Buzz Aldrin successfully completed the first human voyage to the Moon. It was humanity's first step onto a world other than our own, a step accompanied by Armstrong's unforgettable words, "That's one small step for a man, one giant leap for mankind."

SPACE TOURISM TAKES HOLD

In just eight years—from April 12, 1961, until July 20, 1969—outer space changed from a vast unknown into a playground for astronauts from around the world. Most people presumed at that time that the near future of humankind would include space travel for the rest of us.

Excitement and expectation about commercial space travel captured the popular imagination. The seminal 1968 science-fiction film *2001: A Space Odyssey* offered viewers a peek at space travel, complete with an "intelligent" computer that could think like a human. But the film's vision of future spacecraft, while taken to the extreme, didn't seem all that strange. Most people assumed that, thirty years in the future, tens of thousands of people, including private citizens, would be traveling into space on highly advanced craft, perhaps to a Moon colony or a huge floating hotel orbiting the Earth. Major airlines, including Pan Am and TWA, even began taking "reservations" for trips to the Moon. A paltry $5 got you a spot on the waiting list.

It would be a very long wait.

The 1970s, 1980s, and 1990s indeed saw continued manned, government-funded space flights, and the number of professional space travelers grew. The United States and the USSR (and later, the Russian Federation) continued their space exploration efforts with new space launch technologies (the Space Shuttle first blasted off in 1981), new space stations (Skylab, Mir), and advanced orbiting science platforms like the Hubble Space Telescope.

But for the private citizen, space was as distant as it had always been. The incredibly rapid progress of the 1960s Space Race was not repeated in subsequent decades. This was primarily due to poor economic conditions in the United States in the 1970s and in the Soviet Union in the 1980s.

By 1990, the Cold War was ending, and the competitive vigor that had driven the space programs of both superpowers had faded. Space would always be there, people thought, but problems on Earth demanded attention now.

Nevertheless, the desire for private space flight did not disappear. It simply lay dormant, waiting for technology and the will to succeed to catch up with demand. Today, the private space flight industry—independently and in conjunction with government—has the technologies and the expertise to send tourists into space. This is the most exciting time for exploration of the cosmos since Yuri Gagarin's historic flight more than four decades ago. Private companies, using private capital and private-sector know-how, are making space flight a reality for anyone willing to go and able to pay for the trip. New vehicles make space tourism easier, cheaper, and more rewarding, while new spaceports will allow tourists the luxury of departing from numerous locations around the world.

Traveling to space is not exactly a stroll in the park, but it is no longer a journey confined to the imagination, either. Knowledgeable instructors are ready and willing to help, advanced simulators are accessible, spaceports abound, and new spacecraft are making the trip easier and more comfortable than ever before. Even the food is much improved over the freeze-dried everything of old.

By our very nature, human beings have an innate need to explore the unknown. Yes, we can be afraid, but we are not fearful creatures. The desire for knowledge causes fearless babies to crawl around a corner into a new room, bold adolescents to hunger and thirst for new experiences, and countless adults throughout history to sacrifice their lives in the pursuit of new frontiers.

Space exploration is, at heart, the logical and ultimate extension of this very human need for knowledge. Outer space as an idea represents the mysterious and the unknown, the distant past and the far future, where we came from and where we are going. Space also offers the hopeful promise of technological advancement, the possibility of better life for people on Earth (and, someday, beyond Earth), and the search for other life in the Universe.

This final goal—the need to know what else and who else is out there, beyond the boundaries of our tiny planet—is arguably the driving force behind space exploration. Are we alone in the Universe? Or are humans one of dozens, or millions—or billions—of intelligent life forms? The desire to know what is out there will never disappear, and the possible rewards will forever draw humans to take the risks inherent in finding out. And make no mistake: The discovery of another life form in the Universe, if and when it happens, will mark the most important day humankind has ever known.

For all these reasons, millions of people around the world want to go to space themselves. And now, at the dawn of the twenty-first century, the dream has finally become a reality.

SPACE ADVENTURES: YOUR PREMIERE SPACE TRAVEL AGENCY

In 1999, more than 30 years after Neil Armstrong and Buzz Aldrin walked on the Moon, the first segment of the International Space Station (ISS) was launched into orbit.

Also in 1999, Space Adventures of Arlington, Virginia, commissioned a study through the Russian space authorities to report on the possibilities of sending commercial passengers to the International Space Station. The results were promising: According to the Russian authorities, one-week commercial flights to the ISS would be possible, but expensive. The estimated price tag: $20 million per flight.

In early 2000, Space Adventures found an enthusiastic pioneer, a wealthy, 60-year-old California investment manager named Dennis Tito, who had always dreamed of going to space. The company organized a visit to Russia for Tito, where he completed the required medical exams for space flight. His space training process began, and the world welcomed its first space tourist.

A onetime NASA rocket scientist who had worked on solar system exploration systems in the 1960s, Tito became the world's first private space traveler, making the dream a possibility for the rest of us. In one of the largest media events of the year, Dennis Tito climbed aboard a Soyuz rocket that blasted into the heavens on April 28, 2001, from the same launch pad that had sent cosmonaut Yuri Gagarin into space 40 years earlier.

Not long after Tito returned from orbit, Space Adventures met with a second would-be space traveler. This time, the call came from a 28-year-old Internet success story who had wanted to fly to space since his youth.

Over the next year, South African Mark Shuttleworth completed the required training, assembled a series of mission projects, and on April 24, 2002, became the second space tourist and the first African in space. (Like Dennis Tito, Shuttleworth paid $20 million for his eight-day stay aboard the space station.) During the flight, he spoke with former South African president Nelson Mandela and even turned down a marriage proposal from a 14-year-old South African girl.

But with great reward comes risk, and the risks of exploration returned to the fore when the Space Shuttle *Columbia* disintegrated while returning from space on February 1, 2003. Shortly thereafter, the Russian government and Space Adventures postponed plans to send more tourists into space while NASA investigated the disaster. The delay, however, was only temporary. Space agencies, companies, and potential candidates understood and accepted that risk was and always will be part of space travel and that the exploration of space had to continue.

Later in 2003, Space Adventures and Russian officials announced that they would send four new space tourists to the International Space Station over the next four years aboard scheduled Soyuz flights. Further, Space Adventures would plan additional flights and new, fully private missions to the ISS.

Other public figures have publicly spoken about potentially flying to the ISS. For example, supermodel Cindy Crawford reportedly announced that she also wanted to be a space tourist, telling reporters in 2002 that she was considering the $20-million trip to space. Colonel Valery Korzun, the ISS commander at the time, stated that Crawford would be welcomed "with open arms." Other celebrities, including the singer Lance Bass and the actor John Travolta, have also expressed interest in traveling to space.

New orbital and sub-orbital vehicles are now a reality. In October 2004, the privately developed *SpaceShipOne* returned safely from its second sub-orbital flight in less than two weeks, winning the $10-million ANSARI X Prize and demonstrating that commercial space flight is now viable. At the same time, the British conglomerate Virgin announced Virgin Galactic, a new company that plans to begin sending tourists to space in the near future.

Other spacecraft will be built and tested over the next several years, and space travel will soon be affordable for anyone who wants to go to space, not just for millionaires. That's where this book comes in. Before traveling to space, you should know what to expect: where you'll be going, how you'll get there, what you'll accomplish, and how you'll train before launch. You'll also need to know how to live comfortably in orbit, how your day-to-day life will be structured, and how you'll come back to Earth.

The book will also give you a realistic picture of what space travel is like: not the glamorous Hollywood version, but a true understanding of how simple tasks on Earth are accomplished in orbit—things like eating, sleeping, bathing, and going to the bathroom. Life's not always easy in space, but it's certainly interesting. You'll also need to know how to react during an emergency, should one occur during your time in space. The book will help you deal with such contingencies.

Think of this book as a combination travel guide, instruction manual, and survival plan. We hope it will give you a true sense of what space travel is like, from the time you sign on the dotted line to liftoff, and beyond.

WISH YOU WERE HERE:
IMAGES OF A SPACE VACATION

A HURRICANE FORMATION IN THE EARTH'S ATMOSPHERE-- AS ONLY ASTRONAUTS AND SPACE TOURISTS WILL SEE ONE.

THE EARTH'S MOON--AS SEEN FROM THE INTERNATIONAL SPACE STATION.

THE INTERNATIONAL SPACE STATION--TODAY'S PREMIERE SPACE TOURIST DESTINATION.

THESE MOCK-UPS OF MIR MODULES ARE USED AS A TRAINING TOOL FOR ASTRONAUTS AND COSMONAUTS.

THE SOYUZ BOOSTER IS TRANSPORTED TO THE LAUNCH PAD VIA RAIL.

A SOYUZ ROCKET LAUNCHING FROM THE BAIKONUR COSMODROME IN KAZAKHSTAN.

A SOYUZ CAPSULE ON ITS WAY BACK TO EARTH.

CHINA LAUNCHED THEIR FIRST MANNED SPACE FLIGHT MISSION WITH THE SHENZHOU-5 SPACECRAFT.

THE SPACE SHUTTLE ENDEAVOUR.

GETTING THERE IS HALF THE FUN: THE MIG-25 AIRCRAFT CAN REACH ALTITUDES THREE TIMES HIGHER THAN MOUNT EVEREST.

THE COSMOPOLIS XXI (C-21) IS DESIGNED TO JOURNEY TO SUB-ORBITAL SPACE.

SPACESHIPONE MADE PILOTED BACK-TO-BACK FLIGHTS TO WIN THE $10-MILLION ANSARI X PRIZE.

ASTRONAUTS PREPARE FOR A NEUTRAL BUOYANCY SIMULATION.

NEUTRAL BUOYANCY ALLOWS ASTRONAUTS TO EXPERIENCE WEIGHTLESSNESS ON THE SURFACE OF THE EARTH.

THIS ONE-OF-A-KIND EXPERIENCE ALLOWS ASTRONAUTS TO PREPARE FOR THE CONDITIONS OF OUTER SPACE.

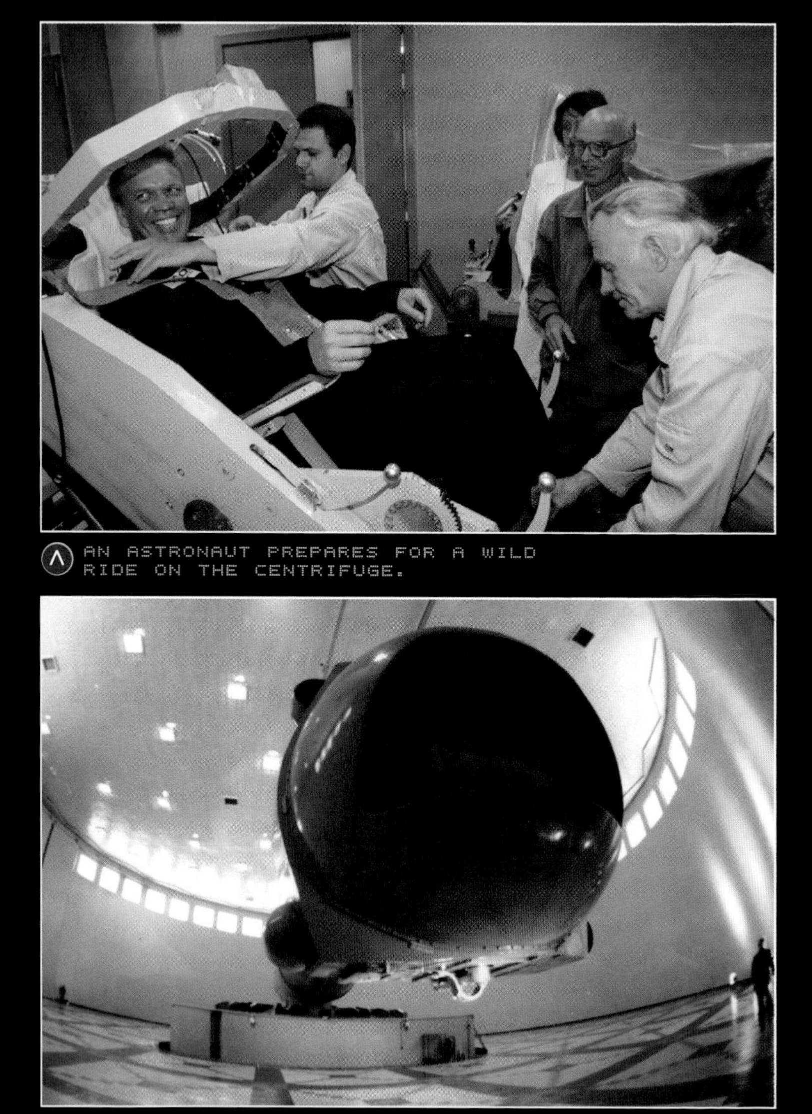

AN ASTRONAUT PREPARES FOR A WILD RIDE ON THE CENTRIFUGE.

CENTRIFUGE TRAINING SIMULATES THE IMMENSE FORCE OF GRAVITY FELT DURING LAUNCH AND REENTRY.

THE SOYUZ SIMULATOR IS USED FOR SPACE FLIGHT COMPUTER TRAINING AND OPERATIONAL SIMULATIONS.

THE CONTROL PANEL OF THE SOYUZ SIMULATOR.

DENNIS TITO MADE HISTORY AS THE FIRST PRIVATE SPACE TOURIST—AND PAVED THE WAY SO OTHERS COULD TRAIN FOR THE VACATION OF A LIFETIME.

WILL YOU BE NEXT?

01: WHERE TO GO: SPACE DESTINATIONS

There are all kinds of space destinations for every kind of budget. In this chapter, we'll look at rewarding places to visit around the globe and throughout the solar system.

GLOBAL SPACEPORTS

Just as cruise ships depart from a handful of specific coastal ports, a journey into space begins from a location geographically suited to the trip: a spaceport.

Global spaceports are the locations on Earth from which space vehicles are launched into orbit. Though located in various countries, traditional spaceports usually share a common trait: Within their respective nations, most are as close to the equator as the country's physical boundaries permit. Because the Earth's rotational velocity is strongest at the equator and weakest at the poles, a space vehicle leaving from the equator (or close to it) benefits from the added "boost" supplied by the planet's rotation. This boost allows the vehicle to carry less fuel than would otherwise be necessary.

KENNEDY SPACE CENTER (FLORIDA, USA)

The Kennedy Space Center (KSC) in Cape Canaveral, Florida, serves as NASA's primary launch facility in the United States. Conveniently located less than 30 minutes from Orlando and Walt Disney World—perfect for pre- or post-flight entertainment—KSC offers a warm, sunny climate from which to begin your space vacation.

Kennedy Space Center is the base for Space Shuttle operations and was the departure site for the first human journey to the Moon. KSC includes the Cape Canaveral Spaceport, Space Shuttle Engineering and Technology programs, and International Space Station payload management and pre-flight assembly operations. KSC also provides technical support to on-orbit operations.

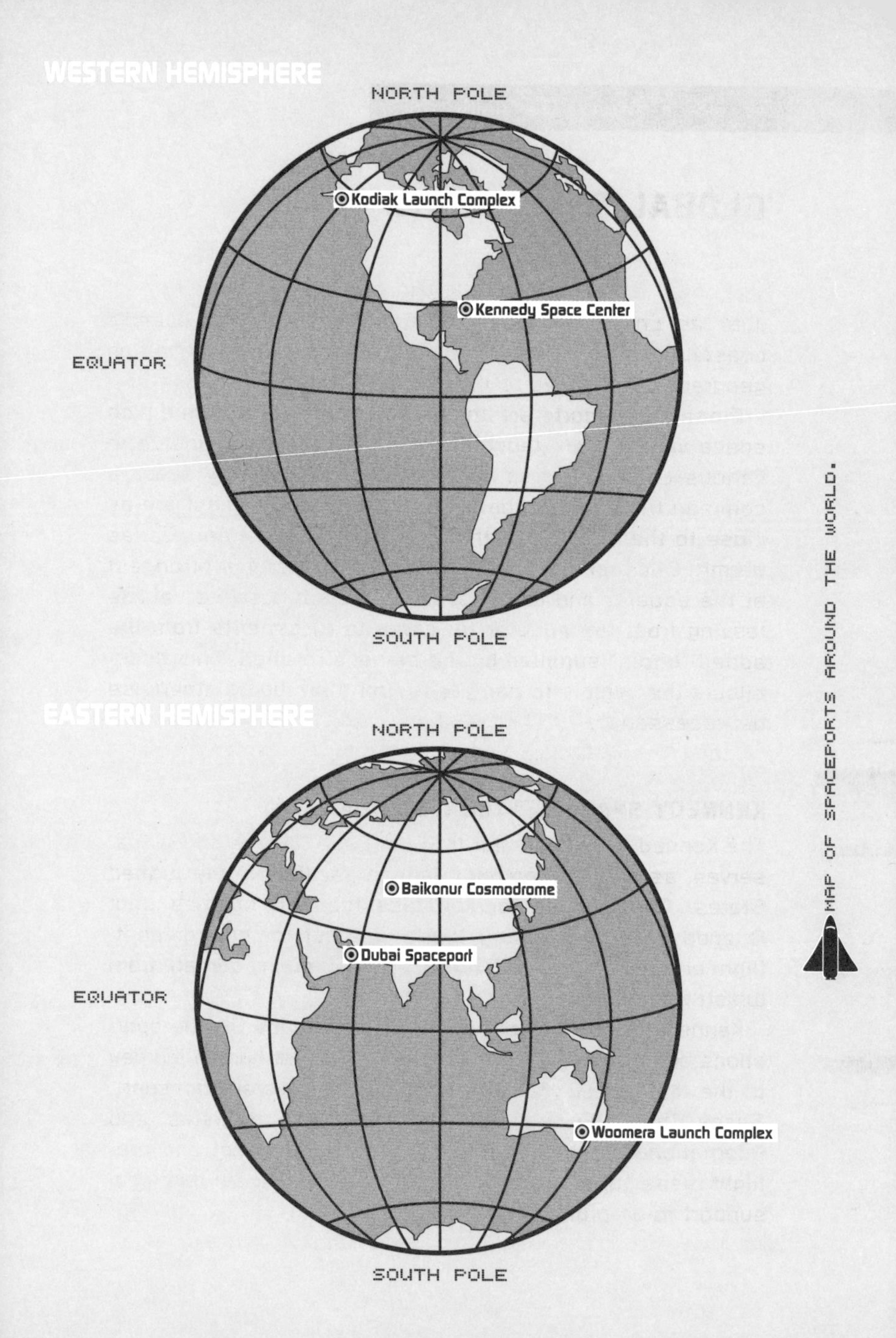
WESTERN HEMISPHERE
NORTH POLE
Kodiak Launch Complex
Kennedy Space Center
EQUATOR
SOUTH POLE
EASTERN HEMISPHERE
NORTH POLE
Baikonur Cosmodrome
Dubai Spaceport
EQUATOR
Woomera Launch Complex
SOUTH POLE
MAP OF SPACEPORTS AROUND THE WORLD.

KODIAK LAUNCH COMPLEX (ALASKA, USA)

Built by the Alaska Aerospace Development Corporation, the launch complex is 25 miles (40.2 km) south of Anchorage on Kodiak Island's Narrow Cape. It is an ideal location for sending space vehicles into polar orbit (see page 80) and therefore does not need to be close to the equator. The Kodiak Launch Complex is a privately run, commercial facility: It offers a basic launch package, which can be customized based on a spacecraft's launch requirements. The complex also has an unobstructed downrange flight path (the northern Pacific Ocean).

The summer climate on Narrow Cape is characterized by relatively cool, comfortable days, with summer temperatures in the 60s and low 70s (15.5–23°C) and rainfall about the same as that on Cape Canaveral. Winter temperatures are in the mid-30s (0–4°C), with about 50 inches (127 cm) of snowfall, on average. Summers feature 18 hours of daylight, while winters feature just six hours. Kodiak Island is a popular hiking and fishing destination during warmer months, but winter visitors should bring a heavy parka.

BAIKONUR COSMODROME (BAIKONUR, KAZAKHSTAN)

Formerly known as Leninsk, Baikonur is the former Soviet and current Russian space center located in south-central Kazakhstan. Founded in 1955, Baikonur is the oldest spaceport in the world. It served as the launch facility for Yuri Gagarin's trip into orbit in 1961, and it is currently used to launch cosmonauts, astronauts, and tourists to the International Space Station. Baikonur is Space Adventures' spaceport of choice; all of the company's orbital missions depart from this location.

Baikonur is situated on the shore of the Syr Darya River in Kazakhstan. The city has a beach and several parks. Because of its northern latitude, the climate in Baikonur is characterized by extremes: Summers are very hot, dry, and windy, with temperatures regularly reaching well above 100°F (37.8°C). Winters, by contrast, are freezing (temperatures may be below 0°F [-17.78°C] for days or weeks at a time) with heavy snowfall from October through March.

Under the Soviets, Baikonur was one of the world's most secret facilities; the area did not even appear on maps until the mid-1990s. The Soviets built the secret city of Leninsk near the facility to provide apartments, schools, and administrative support to the tens of thousands of workers at the launch facility.

The Baikonur Cosmodrome supports a wide range of launch vehicles, including Soyuz, Proton, Tsyklon, Dnepr, and Zenit. With several launch pads operational for both manned and unmanned missions, Baikonur is the most active launch site in the world. The facility also plays an essential role in the deployment and routine operation of the International Space Station.

WOOMERA LAUNCH COMPLEX (WOOMERA, AUSTRALIA)

A spaceport and space flight training center for suborbital programs is currently planned to be constructed at the Woomera launch range in Southern Australia; the complex should be complete in late 2006 or 2007. Woomera is one of the least accessible and hottest places on Earth: Summer temperatures can reach 120°F (48.9°C), while winters are generally 50–60°F (10–16°C) during daylight hours and cold at night. Visitors in summer should bring a hat with a broad brim, sunglasses, and plenty of sunscreen, as well as loose-fitting clothing. A light jacket is recommended, as even summer evenings can be cool and breezy. The town of Woomera has several hotels, a golf course, a swimming pool, tennis courts, and a ten-pin bowling alley. Popular day trips include hikes into the Southern Australia Outback and visits to the town observatory and the missile park, which features various types of rockets and jets.

Woomera has been used as a rocket and ballistic missile development and testing facility since the end of World War II and was also used by NASA as a deep-space tracking station until 1990. Future plans for Woomera include testing of Next Generation Supersonic Transport Project prototypes and a launch facility for space tourists.

Like Baikonur, Woomera was surrounded by a secret town closed to the outside world. The town of Woomera Village was opened by the Australian government in 1982 and is now accessible to tourists.

DUBAI SPACEPORT (DUBAI, UNITED ARAB EMIRATES)

Many private investors are now considering Dubai as a prime location for a new global spaceport. The UAE's clear skies, predictable climate and weather patterns, and proximity to the equator make it a highly attractive candidate for a launch facility. Dubai is also becoming a true tourist destination: A huge underwater park ("Hydropolis") is under construction, a large man-made island is being built, and there are numerous beaches and luxury hotels. The Dubai Spaceport is likely to be used exclusively by space tourists.

DESTINATIONS IN SPACE

Spaceports on Earth are gateways to destinations above, making the universe your playground. Here are some places you might consider visiting.

INTERNATIONAL SPACE STATION

The ultimate orbital destination for space tourists in the decade to come will be the International Space Station (ISS), a floating "apartment complex" with numerous activity areas and observation posts for vacationers to enjoy. Though the station is not scheduled for completion until at least 2006 (it has been operating with full crews since 2000), you won't have to worry about excessive construction noise or debris: The ISS is highly compartmentalized, and new sections (called "modules") are designed and built on Earth, then connected to the existing platform in orbit.

More than four times as large as the Russian Mir space station that it replaced, the completed International Space Station will be 356 feet (108 m) across and 290 feet (88 m) long (slightly larger than a football field), with nearly an acre of solar panels to provide electrical power to six scientific laboratories.

The ISS orbits at an altitude of about 250 miles (402.3 km), in a location that allows the station to be reached by supply vehicles launched from geographically disparate spaceports, including the Baikonur Cosmodrome and Kennedy Space Center. The current orbit also provides excellent opportunities for Earth observation.

The largest and most complex international scientific project in history, the ISS draws upon the scientific and technological resources of 16 nations. Currently, the United

States has responsibility for developing and ultimately operating the major elements and systems aboard the station. The ISS offers visitors a vast array of on-orbit activities, including the chance to conduct scientific experiments in the research module, test the cellular effects of radiation in the Biolab, and sleep, eat, and shower in the permanent habitation module.

While staying at the International Space Station, tourists can also view, operate, or visit other modules and devices being developed by numerous countries.

- Canada is providing a 55-foot (17 m) robotic arm to be used for assembly and maintenance tasks at the Space Station.
- The European Space Agency is building a pressurized laboratory to be launched on the Space Shuttle and logistics transport vehicles to be launched on the Ariane 5 launch vehicle.
- Japan is building a laboratory with an attached, exposed exterior platform for experiments, as well as logistics transport vehicles.
- Russia has provided two research modules; the service module, with its own life support and habitation systems; a power platform of solar arrays that can supply about 20 kilowatts of electrical power; logistics transport vehicles; and Soyuz spacecraft for crew return and transfer.

PRIVATE SPACE STATIONS

Several companies are currently developing private space stations and other nongovernmental space habitats. These commercial, for-profit enterprises are privately funded and are likely to play an important role in future space tourism.

The idea behind private space stations is simple: Governments (and government-controlled aerospace contractors) have neither the ability nor the desire to make space travel available for the paying consumer—costs and risks are too high, and benefits too low. Only through private investment will private citizens be able to enjoy the benefits of space travel.

One company in particular, Bigelow Aerospace, intends to make commercial space destinations a reality in the near future. Through the use of low-volume, lightweight inflatable space modules, Bigelow hopes to create a habitable space environment at a fraction of the cost of current technology. The company's Genesis Pathfinder is a prototype design for an inflatable space habitat based on TransHab, a similar project created but later abandoned by NASA. If a planned 2006 test of Genesis is successful, work on the full-size Nautilus inflatable module will begin.

The journey to Nautilus is likely to be made with a reusable launch vehicle, with a travel time of two to three days from launch to docking. Once there, your activities are likely to include floating, stargazing, and taking pictures, as well as the challenging acts of eating and bathing in a microgravity environment.

Space travelers who plan to visit a private space station should keep a few pertinent accommodation facts in mind. When fully inflated in space, Nautilus will be just 45 feet (13.7 m) long and 22 feet (6.7 m) in diameter, hundreds of feet smaller than the ISS. Such dimensions mean that quarters would be tight on an inflatable private space station, so "private time" will be minimal. Consider bringing someone you love—not just a friend or acquaintance—on this very intimate journey.

L5

L5, technically known as the fifth Lagrangian Libration point, offers a tantalizing yet currently purely theoretical destination for space tourists. Lagrangian Libration points are precise locations part way between two celestial bodies, such as the Earth and the Moon or the Sun and the Earth, where a spacecraft or space station would always remain in the same position with respect to both entities. (In a traditional geosynchronous Earth orbit, an object stays in the same fixed position relative to the Earth, but not to the Moon or other celestial bodies.)

Though there are five such points, research has shown that a space station located at or near L5 would remain in a fixed position (relative to the Earth and the Moon) at a low

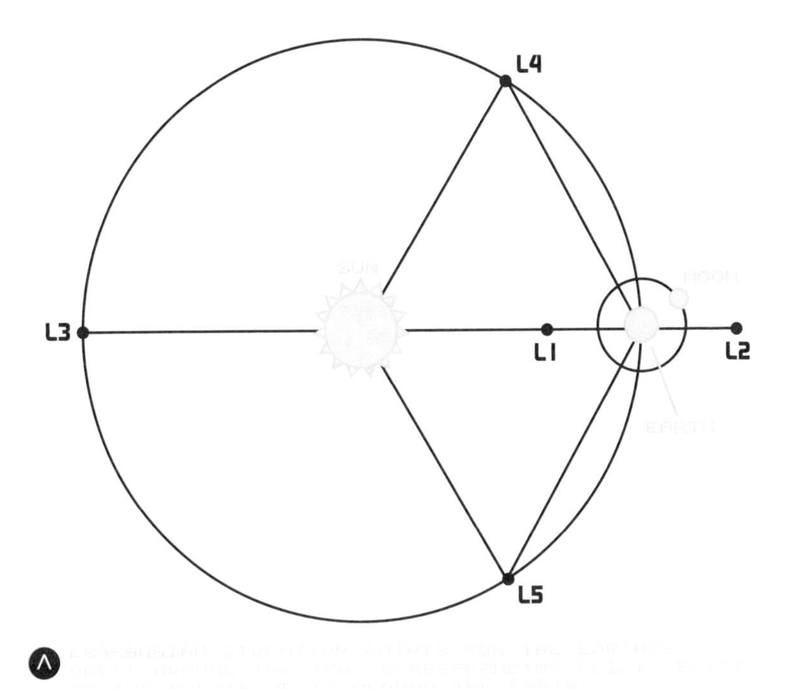

LAGRANGIAN LIBRATION POINTS FOR THE EARTH'S ORBIT AROUND THE SUN. CORRESPONDING POINTS EXIST ON THE MOON'S ORBIT AROUND THE EARTH.

orbit of about 90,000 feet (27 km). Manufacturing facilities located at L5 could produce cheap energy through the use of solar power satellites, using resources from the Moon or asteroids. The energy produced at L5 could be delivered to Earth via microwaves, and scientists have estimated that dozens of such "super-satellites" could meet the present electrical needs of the entire United States.

A study by NASA in the 1970s concluded that, conceptually, constructing a settlement at L5 was possible by 1990, using discarded fuel tanks from the Space Shuttle. The tanks would be refurbished and connected to form a huge, hollow ring, which would form the outer shell of a space station that could house 3,000 people. However, assumptions about the frequency of shuttle flights (60 per year) later proved too optimistic, funding for research into solar satellites was cut, and official NASA support for the concept ended. Though highly theoretical, commercial development at L5 is currently promoted by the L5 Society.

THE MOON

A space tourist is probably more likely to eventually land on the Moon than on any other celestial body (aside from space stations). Though costs are currently prohibitive, the Moon's relative proximity to the Earth, its history of exploration by humans, our ability to reach it using current technology, and the presence of ice and valuable minerals all point to a future when visits to the Moon will be unexceptional, if not commonplace.

Visits to the Moon are likely to be for one of two reasons: tourism or commercial energy production. The first step in Moon travel could be the construction of a Moon base, using lunar materials. Using solar power, water could be melted from Moon ice and then mixed with lunar dust to form "lunar cement." Alternatively, Moon dust might be combined with a polymer (shipped from Earth) to form a castable material that could be formed into building blocks or bricks.

Some advocates believe that a robot Moon base will be constructed by 2015 and a human base by 2020. Indeed, in 2004, U.S. president George W. Bush instructed NASA to begin planning a return trip to the Moon as the first step in the construction of a Moon base, which will then be used as a way station on the first manned mission to Mars.

The Moon's low gravity (about one-sixth that of Earth) could aid in the construction of buildings, but residents and visitors will need to be shielded from the Sun's radiation, either by thick walls or by living beneath the lunar surface. The presence of ice on the Moon (NASA estimates 6.6 billion tons [6 billion metric tons]) means that there is likely to be a sufficient supply of potable water, crucial to the survival of any human settlement.

A stay on the Moon is likely to be significantly different from a trip to a space station. For one thing, the presence of gravity (albeit greatly reduced from Earth's gravity) means that you would be able to walk (or "hop") on the lunar surface, as well as drive a vehicle to more distant locales. Other activities might include planting a flag, collecting rock samples, taking photos, visiting large craters, and making a day trip to the "dark side" of the Moon. Of course, such trips, unlike the shirtsleeve environment found on space stations, would require a complete extravehicular spacesuit.

Unfortunately, using current orbital launch vehicle technologies, the cost of constructing and operating a Moon base may prove prohibitive for commercial entities, and perhaps even for governments; estimates run into the tens of billions of dollars. Thus, Moon tourism over the next decade is likely to be limited to weeklong stays on a lunar cruiser orbiting the Moon's surface (see page 82).

>> SAMPLE MOON VISIT ITINERARY

DAY[S]	ACTIVITY
1–3	Travel to Moon.
4–5	Arrival. Welcome glass of Moon Punch. Acclimation to low gravity. Meet and greet Moon-based support staff ("Moonies"). Short, brisk walk on lunar surface.
6	Longer Moon walk. Rock sample collecting.
7	Free day. Send e-mail using Moon computers. Take photographs of the Moon base. Enjoy a buffet dinner with other astronauts. Indulge in savory Moon pies.
8	Daylong hike to "highlands" and other major craters.
9	Prepare for departure. Pack souvenirs. E-mail your photos. Visit clinic for preflight enema.
10	Departure. Return to Earth.

WHEN VISITING THE MOON, BE SURE TO BRING THE FLAG OF YOUR NATIVE COUNTRY. ^

02: HOW TO GET THERE: SPACE VEHICLES

Departing for space isn't like hopping a last-minute flight to Chicago or Sydney. There are numerous types of spacecraft, and each has its own unique set of mission parameters, its own specific crew and tourist capacity, and its own launch and reentry experience. Today's space adventurer has a fairly broad array of transport vehicles available, with more expected over the next decade. Some space vehicles are capable of reaching only the lowest edge of space (the upper atmosphere), while others are designed specifically to be launched into orbit and sub-orbit. The type of vehicle you use will be determined by your choice of space mission.

EDGE-OF-SPACE AIRCRAFT

Planes with conventional jet engines capable of very high-altitude flight (known as a "high ceiling") but that do not actually enter orbit are known as "edge-of-space" aircraft. These planes, usually high-performance fighter jets, can reach altitudes of about 80,000 feet (24.3 km) and speeds in excess of Mach 2 (twice the speed of sound).

MiG-25

As a straight-line fighter designed for high-altitude, high-speed operations, the MiG-25 is the ideal aircraft to take space travelers on their first journey above 99.9 percent of the Earth's atmosphere, to the "edge of space."

The MiG-25 is a twin-finned high-wing monoplane with slightly swept wings, a variable-angle tail, lateral air intakes, and two Tumanski R-31 turbojet engines with full afterburners. It is currently the fastest combat aircraft ever built, capable of reaching speeds slightly above Mach 2.8.

The airframe of the MiG-25 is built largely of steel to resist

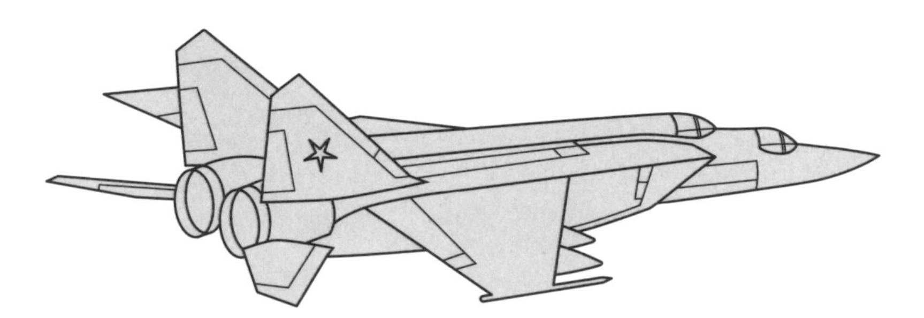

the high temperatures developed by air friction at high speeds; a titanium skin protects all critical leading edges and joints that are subjected to excessive temperatures. Your seat inside the plane, directly behind the pilot, will be snug but comfortable, with its own ejection system (the pilot can also eject you, if necessary). Though the seat back will not recline and there is no tray table, you will have enough storage space to bring a small camera. Your helmet will include an oxygen mask and a communications system so you can speak with your pilot during the trip. (See page 70 for more details on this trip.)

The MiG-25 is currently in service in Russia, Ukraine, and India, and is operated commercially for space tourism by Space Adventures.

F-104

The F-104 is a military aircraft used by several nations as an air-defense interceptor and fighter-bomber. Due to its relatively short range, it is no longer used by the U.S. military, but several space tourism operators (including Space Adventures) use it for high-altitude training experiences: Its numerous speed, altitude, and time-to-climb records make it

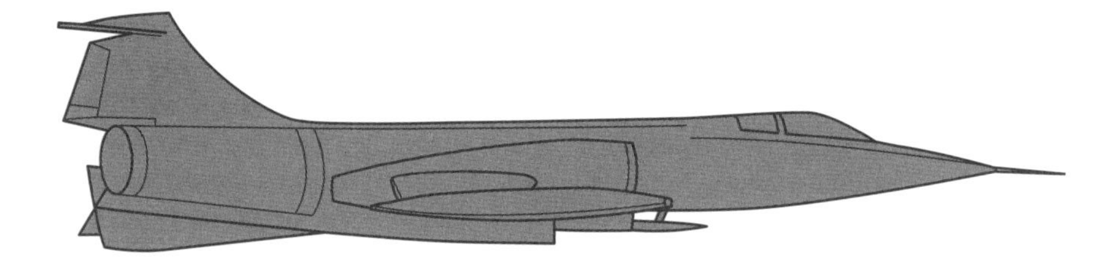

an ideal choice for a trip to the edge of space. Additionally, the F-104's unique capabilities allow effective simulation of vertical launch maneuvers (G-forces, weightlessness) over short distances and for short time periods. The F-104 can simulate the initial 30–40 seconds of launch forces of the Soyuz rocket (page 59) and the NASA Space Shuttles (page 58).

SUB-ORBITAL SYSTEMS

Although edge-of-space aircraft can bring you to a maximum altitude of about 15 miles (24.1 km), sub-orbital spacecraft travel to space itself, which is generally defined as 62 miles (100 km) altitude. Astronauts and ships entering this region are truly "in space" and experience weightlessness for an extended period of time.

There are currently several different sub-orbital Reusable Launch Vehicle (RLV) designs in early production or development. Some launch from a runway like an airplane, accelerating to about Mach 4, and zoom up to above 60 miles (96.5 km) before recovering and landing on Earth in much the same way as a Space Shuttle lands.

Other craft include two-stage designs. The first stage includes a standard jet aircraft, which carries a rocket-powered lifting body to around 50,000 feet (15.24 km). The lifting body then separates from the aircraft, accelerates to around Mach 5, and zooms to above 60 miles (96.5 km). Reentries are also similar to the Space Shuttle's, with landing either by parachute or runway. The occupants will be weightless during the parabolic portion of the flight trajectory, from engine shutdown until deceleration back to the Earth's atmosphere. The duration of these flights depends on the spacecraft, but in general, the entire trip will take about an hour, and weightlessness will last for several minutes.

SPACESHIPONE

On June 22, 2004, the first human space vehicle developed entirely with private funds launched successfully into space and returned to Earth safely. This launch of *SpaceShipOne* (*SS1*) was followed by two more, one in late September

2004 and the second a week later, which resulted in the awarding of the coveted $10-million ANSARI X Prize to *SpaceShipOne*'s creators.

Conceived by legendary aircraft designer Burt Rutan and funded by Microsoft cofounder and billionaire Paul Allen, *SpaceShipOne* was first proposed in 1996. A full development program began in strict secrecy in April 2001, inspired by the X Prize and the space flight of Dennis Tito, also in April of that year.

With the milestone launches in 2004, *SS1* demonstrated that future space tourism for the general public could be made affordable by a fully private "space program."

FLIGHT PROFILE

SpaceShipOne is a three-sectioned spacecraft attached to a turbojet launch aircraft called *White Knight*, which climbs for an hour to 50,000 feet (15.24 km). Designer Burt Rutan considered ground-level rocket launches too risky and inefficient. (For a sub-orbital flight, a ground-launched ship must be twice the weight of one launched from 50,000 feet.)

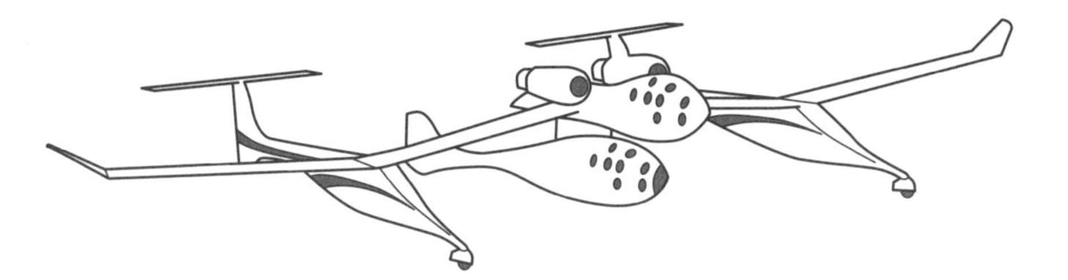

SpaceShipOne is then dropped from *White Knight* and fires its rocket motor while climbing steeply for more than a minute, reaching a speed of 2,500 mph (4,023 km/h). The ship coasts up to an altitude of 62 miles (100 km), and then falls back into the atmosphere after about three minutes in space. During weightless flight, the spaceship converts to a high-drag configuration (similar to a badminton shuttlecock) to allow a safe, stable atmospheric entry.

After the one-minute entry deceleration, the ship converts back to a conventional glider, allowing a leisurely 17-minute glide from 80,000 feet (24.4 km) down to the runway, where a landing is made at lower speeds.

The unique configuration of the *White Knight* and *SpaceShipOne* allows aircraft-like qualities of boost, glide, and landing.

FLIGHT ACCOMMODATIONS

Designed for a "shirtsleeve" environment (no space suit required), *SpaceShipOne* has a small cabin with tiny dual-pane windows. Accommodations on *SS1* include a seat for a pilot and two passenger seats (though future versions may accommodate several tourists), with views in multiple directions from the ship's "portal" windows. The windows are kept small to reduce weight and are round to minimize structural loads. Each portal consists of two windows to provide redundancy for the integrity of the cabin, should one window crack or fail. The number and location of the windows provide the occupants a view of the horizon throughout *SpaceShipOne*'s mission profile. Tourist flights on future versions are expected to last one to two hours.

SpaceShipOne makes use of a new GPS navigation system that provides the pilot with the precise guidance information he needs to manually fly the spacecraft for boost and reentry. It also provides guidance for approach and landing and vehicle systems monitoring.

Perhaps the most technologically controversial area of the *SpaceShipOne* system is its hybrid rocket motor. This liquid NO_2 oxidizer and rubber-fuel hybrid propulsion system was developed specifically for *SpaceShipOne* and had never been used for a manned space flight system. Though the design simplifies mounting, reduces leak paths, and has the advantage of using fairly inert fuel and oxidizers, the long-term reliability of the solid/liquid combination is unclear.

XERUS

Built by XCOR Aerospace of Mojave, California, the Xerus will carry one passenger and one pilot into space. Xerus has been designed to operate efficiently at the lowest possible operational cost. It will be powered by XCOR's own rocket engines, which have already demonstrated long life and a very low operational cost. The Xerus will provide an "Alan Shepard–style" ride: a quick and exhilarating boost to an altitude of 62 miles (100 km), with about three minutes of zero gravity and a terrific view of the Earth. In zero gravity, tourists might briefly float around the cabin or perform flips and rolls. A small snack will probably be served, but be sure to hold on to your pretzels, or they will float freely in the spacecraft until the ship reenters the atmosphere. Beverage service, however, is likely to be messy and will probably not be available.

Wings provide for runway takeoffs and landings, as well as maneuvering in the atmosphere. Small rockets are used for attitude control outside the atmosphere. Initial flight-testing will retain a propellant reserve so that the pilot can restart the engines to reach the airport or perform a go-around if necessary. XCOR plans a test flight program of at least 20 flights, each building on the flight plan of the one that came before.

COSMOPOLIS XXI (C-21)

The C-21 reusable space tourism system is being designed and produced by the same Russian Design Bureau that designed the Russian Space Shuttle *Buran* in the late 1980s and early 1990s. The C-21 is being conceived wholly for space tourism and is able to carry out a sub-orbital flight with a three-person crew (two passengers plus a pilot). The spacecraft, with a physical design reminiscent of the U.S. Space Shuttles, is likely to be a bit more spacious than *SpaceShipOne*, though it shares that ship's general flight profile. Tourist flights are likely to last one to two hours and include some "float" time in space, as well as plenty of time for picture taking.

The complete system consists of an M-55 carrier aircraft together with the C-21 three-seat sub-orbital Reusable Launch Vehicle (RLV), equipped with a rocket booster and life support, control, and recovery systems. The RLV is installed above the aircraft fuselage using special attachment points.

After takeoff, the carrier aircraft climbs to 11.8 miles (19 km) and accelerates to perform the zooming maneuver. At the proper altitude and trajectory, the carrier aircraft performs the breakaway maneuver; the RLV's rocket booster fires, beginning its climb. The RLV continues its ballistic flight to an altitude of about 62 miles (100 km). The RLV then performs a ballistic descent with body braking and deceleration by parachutes, leading to a glider landing.

ROCKETPLANE XP

The Rocketplane XP is being designed and fabricated in Oklahoma City by Rocketplane Limited. The spaceplane is designed to carry a pilot, copilot, and up to three passengers on sub-orbital space flights to 62 miles (100 km) altitude or higher.

The fighter-sized spaceplane is powered by two 3,000-pound (1,361 kg) thrust turbojet engines and a single 30,000-pound (13,608 kg) thrust rocket engine. The patented ORBITEC Vortex Combustion Cold-Wall Chamber engine reduces cost, weight, and complexity while increasing engine lifetime, reliability, and performance. Liquid oxygen and kerosene are the main fuel for a simple and reliable pressure-fed propellant system. The XP uses safe, already-certified aircraft components and assembly/maintenance practices and takes an incremental approach to flight testing. To assure safety and reliability, the Rocketplane employs modern fly-by-wire technology and redundant flight control computers and avionics.

The XP does not use any launch-assist or carrier aircraft. It takes off under its own jet power and flies in subsonic cruise to the designated rocket ignition point. The spaceplane then immediately performs a 3-G pull-up maneuver and climbs at a 75-degree angle to speeds of more than 1,500 mph (2,414 km/h). After a main engine burn of about 90 seconds, the rocket engine is shut off, and the plane coasts upward to an altitude of more than 330,000 feet (100.6 km). At maximum altitude, the spaceplane performs a slow roll to permit tourists to see and enjoy the full panorama of the Earth below. The flight crew and passengers experience up to four minutes of weightlessness as the XP reaches its highest altitude and begins to descend.

Atmospheric reentry begins at about 150,000 feet (45.72 km) altitude. During the minute or so of peak deceleration from above Mach 3 to subsonic speed, deceleration forces build up to a peak of more than 4 Gs. Once a subsonic cruise glide is established, the jet engines are restarted for a powered approach to the runway.

The XP uses a proprietary thermal protection coating on the nose cap and leading edges to handle the heat caused by reentry. The Rocketplane also has a cold gas thruster system for maneuvering the vehicle while outside the atmosphere. Window and door seals and life support systems are dually redundant, so passengers are not required to wear bulky helmets and pressure suits that are uncomfortable and limit visibility.

Multiple onboard cameras (both internal and external) and digital video recorders will capture the entire experience, while real-time downlinks to Mission Control will permit friends and relatives of the Rocketplane space tourists to watch and enjoy the space flight too. Flying mixed payloads is also possible, with passengers conducting microgravity experiments as part of their mission plan.

MiG-31 DERIVATIVES

Several academicians at the Moscow Institute of Aviation have proposed a new, relatively inexpensive launch system that would allow space tourists to experience a brief suborbital space flight.

A new type of booster rocket, powering a small spacecraft, would be released from the bottom of a MiG-31 fighter jet and would proceed into space after separation from the aircraft and ignition. One benefit of this system is relatively low development costs, since the carrier aircraft (the MiG) already exists and would probably need only minor modifications.

Minutes after separation from the MiG carrier aircraft, up to three tourists and their pilot would reach an altitude of 62 miles (100 km), experience weightlessness for two to four minutes, and view the Earth from a small window in the spacecraft. Unlike *SpaceShipOne* and other glider-based designs, Earth return on this spacecraft would be achieved by a wing-like parafoil parachute that would deploy high above the Earth's surface. Tourists would enjoy a leisurely float back to land with dramatic views of the planet below.

ORBITAL SYSTEMS

Orbital spacecraft are the true space vehicles: These ships leave the atmosphere far behind as they reach altitudes of 100–200 miles (161–322 km) and orbit the Earth. Orbital vehicles are capable of extended periods in space, from two weeks (for the Space Shuttle) to months and years for orbiting platforms like the International Space Station.

SPACE SHUTTLE

Might space tourists someday reach orbit aboard a Space Shuttle, perhaps operated by a private company in conjunction with NASA? The possibility is tantalizing: The shuttle can accommodate eight guests, includes sleeping quarters, and is capable of two weeks in orbit. A shuttle tourist might also be able to observe a science mission or ride the ship to the ISS.

A trip on the shuttle is highly dramatic. The Space Shuttle system is a reusable, three-engine, winged spacecraft (the "orbiter") attached to two solid rocket boosters and a large external tank for launch. The boosters provide the main thrust to lift the orbiter off the launch pad, while the external tank supplies fuel and oxidizer to the Space Shuttle's main engines during launch. The Space Shuttle reaches a speed of about 17,000 mph (27,358 km/h) approximately eight minutes after launch. On reentry, the shuttle lands on a conventional runway, deploying parachutes to decelerate.

The Space Shuttle Orbiter supports a crew of eight and is capable of extended periods in space: A typical flight is 10 days, with a maximum of about 16 days. In addition to its capacity as a laboratory for scientific experiments conducted while in orbit, the Space Shuttle has served as a supply vehicle for the International Space Station (ISS) and, using a robotic arm or astronauts on spacewalks, as a repair vehicle for satellites and the Hubble Space Telescope.

The Space Shuttle program is owned by the United States government and administered by NASA. Though there has been no indication from NASA that its fleet of orbiters will be made available for space tourism, the shuttle is not without value for space tourism operators. Several new spacecraft designs (including the C-21) are loosely based on the orbiter model, which is a proven vessel and offers the distinct advantage of a runway landing—the preferred method used by today's ship designers.

In addition, the loss of the shuttle *Columbia* in 2003 has led to setbacks in the Space Shuttle program, including a sharply reduced flight schedule. The shuttle program is scheduled to be phased out in 2010, to be replaced by some type of reusable launch vehicle that is cheaper to launch and maintain.

SOYUZ-FG LAUNCH VEHICLE AND -TMA SPACECRAFT

If you want to go orbital right now, your most viable option is aboard a Soyuz-TMA spacecraft. This vehicle blasts into space atop a huge rocket called the Soyuz-FG launch vehicle. High above the Earth, the spacecraft modules separate from the rocket, and tourists (at this point official astronauts) enjoy unobstructed views of the entire planet, hours or days of weightlessness, and perhaps a visit to the ISS.

The Soyuz-FG is a three-stage launching system. The system includes a lower portion, with four first-stage boosters and a central core for the second stage, and an upper portion (the third stage), which includes a payload adapter and payload faring.

Liquid oxygen (LOX) and kerosene are used as propellants in all three Soyuz stages. For tourists, this particular combination of propellants is highly desirable. The mixture is a proven rocket propellant that offers the added benefit of relative safety: LOX itself does not burn but rather is an oxidizer that supports the vigorous combustion of a flammable fuel like kerosene. The LOX/kerosene combination has been used successfully in rockets since the earliest days of the space program.

There have been more than 1,600 launches using the Soyuz family of launchers, and mission parameters have included satellite launches, Earth observation, weather and scientific experiments, and human flights. Soyuz missions are launched from the Baikonur Cosmodrome in Kazakhstan. Space Adventures uses the Soyuz-FG launch vehicle for its space tourist flights to the ISS, and the Soyuz has earned its reputation as the most reliable manned space flight system in history.

The Soyuz-TMA spacecraft is designed to serve as the International Space Station's crew return vehicle, acting as a lifeboat in the event an emergency requires immediate evacuation. A new Soyuz capsule is normally delivered to the station every six months. A Soyuz spacecraft generally takes two days after launch to reach the Space Station.

Fortunately, there is no need for you to master a complicated series of commands and controls. For your convenience, once you reach the ISS, rendezvous and docking are both completely automated. Once the spacecraft is within 492 feet (150 m) of the station, the Russian Mission Control Center just outside Moscow monitors the approach and docking. The Soyuz crew has the capability to manually intervene or execute these operations if necessary.

The Soyuz-TMA spacecraft consists of three sections: an orbital module, a descent module, and an instrumentation/propulsion module.

ORBITAL MODULE

Upon reaching orbit, you and the crew will slowly move ("float") from the descent module (which is also where you sit during launch) to the orbital module. The Soyuz orbital module will be your "home" in orbit, at least until you reach the ISS. It has a volume of 230 cubic feet (6.5 cubic m), with a docking mechanism, hatch, and rendezvous antennas located at the front end. The docking mechanism is used to dock with the Space Station, and the hatch allows easy entry into the station. The rendezvous antennas are used by the radar-based automated docking system to maneuver the module toward the station for docking. There is also a window in the module, though the best views are likely to be from the descent module, which has two windows.

The opposite end of the orbital module connects to the descent module via a pressurized hatch. Before you return to Earth, you will move back through the hatch to the descent module, which will then separate from the orbital and propulsion modules and return to Earth (below).

DESCENT MODULE

The descent module is where you and your crewmates sit for launch, reentry, and landing and is the only portion of the Soyuz-TMA that survives the return to Earth. This module includes all necessary controls and displays for the Soyuz-TMA, as well as life support supplies, batteries used during descent, primary and backup parachutes, and landing rockets.

The seats in the module (sometimes known as "Kazbek couches") contain custom-fitted seat liners for each crewmember: Each is individually molded to the occupant's body to ensure a tight, comfortable fit. (When crewmembers are brought to the station aboard the Soyuz-TMA, their seat liners are delivered with them and transferred to the existing Soyuz lifeboat spacecraft as part of crew handover activities.) Though the seats do not recline (and don't include a flip-out movie screen), your seat liner should be snug and reasonably supportive.

The descent module's eight hydrogen peroxide thrusters control the spacecraft's orientation, or attitude, during descent until parachute deployment. The module also has a guidance, navigation, and control system to maneuver the vehicle during descent. The module includes a periscope, which allows you to view the docking target on the station or the Earth below.

The module has a habitable volume of 141 cubic feet (4 cubic m), not much bigger than a midsize bathroom. Approximately 110 pounds (50 kg) of cargo ("payload") can be returned to Earth in the module.

INSTRUMENTATION/PROPULSION MODULE

This third and final module contains three compartments: intermediate, instrumentation, and propulsion.

The intermediate compartment is where this module connects to the descent module. It also contains oxygen storage tanks and the attitude control thrusters, as well as electronics, communications, and control equipment. The primary guidance, navigation, control, and computer systems of the Soyuz are in the instrumentation compartment, which is a sealed container filled with circulating nitrogen gas to cool the avionics equipment. Though you will not be able to enter this compartment, ask your mission commander to explain the various control mechanisms and how they work.

The propulsion compartment contains the primary thermal control system and the Soyuz radiator. The propulsion system, batteries, solar arrays, and structural connection to the Soyuz launch rocket are located in this compartment. The propulsion compartment also contains the system that is used to perform any maneuvers while in orbit, including rendezvous and docking with the Space Station and the deorbit burns necessary to return to Earth.

The two Soyuz solar arrays are attached to either side of the rear section of the instrumentation/propulsion module and are linked to rechargeable batteries. Like the orbital module, the intermediate section of the instrumentation/propulsion module separates from the descent module after the final deorbit maneuver and burns up in atmosphere upon reentry.

SOYUZ LANDING

Up to three crewmembers can return from the International Space Station aboard a Soyuz-TMA spacecraft. The vehicle lands on the flat steppes of Kazakhstan in central Asia. A Soyuz trip to the station takes two days from launch to docking because many orbits are necessary to bring the craft to the altitude and speed of the ISS. The return to Earth, by contrast, takes less than four hours.

The Soyuz commander can pilot the descent module using a rotational hand controller that manages the firing of the eight hydrogen peroxide thrusters on the vehicle's exterior. This system is deactivated 15 minutes before landing, when the parachutes are deployed.

Having shed two-thirds of its mass, the Soyuz reaches entry interface—a point 400,000 feet (12.19 km) above the Earth, where friction due to the thickening atmosphere begins to heat the module's outer surfaces—three hours after undocking. With only 23 minutes left before the Soyuz lands in central Asia, attention in the module turns to slowing its rate of descent.

Eight minutes later, the spacecraft is streaking through the sky at 755 feet (230 m) per second. The G-loads will make breathing labored, and you will feel pressure on your legs and torso. Before it touches down, the module's speed slows to 5 feet (1.5 m) per second, and it lands at an even lower speed after four parachutes are deployed. When the drogue and main chutes are fired, out and away from the module, you will feel sharp jerks as the speeding craft suddenly loses velocity. One second before touchdown, two sets of three small engines on the bottom of the module will fire, slowing the vehicle to soften the landing.

SHENZHOU

In the near future, space tourists may have the option of blasting into orbit aboard a new class of rocket from China called the Shenzhou. Although the Chinese-built "Long March" launch system has had some problems over the last decade, the initial performance of Shenzhou has been superb, and it has become an attractive candidate for tourist flights to space. The overall launch and flight characteristics are similar to those of the Soyuz.

The Chinese Shenzhou is a three-module orbiter designed to be launched into space atop a Long March 2F booster rocket. Using a Shenzhou-5 (the fifth version after four test flights), China sent its first astronaut into orbit in October 2003, marking the country's first successful manned space flight; astronaut Yang Liwei was given the title "Space Hero" upon his return to Earth.

The Shenzhou's three modules include an ascent/descent module for the crew, an orbital module for science equipment, and a service module with solar panels, electronics, and rocket engines. The Shenzhou is capable of carrying three crewmembers but to date has housed only one.

Though widely believed to be based on a Soyuz design, the Shenzhou has a feature not found on the Soyuz. The forward module on the Shenzhou can remain in orbit unmanned, where it can be piloted remotely and conduct experiments after its astronaut has returned to Earth. There is speculation that, in the future, multiple orbiting modules might be connected to form a new space station.

A recent aerospace technology-sharing agreement between China and Russia may result in improved spacecraft for both countries. These jointly developed vehicles could someday ferry many space tourists into orbit.

>> A GUIDE TO SYMBOLS

The following symbols are used throughout this chapter to help you determine the affordability of a vacation package. Note that prices may vary based on the mission parameters of your particular trip.

$	**Inexpensive (less than $10,000)**
$$	**Moderate ($10,000–$50,000)**
$$$	**Expensive ($50,000–$200,000)**
$$$$	**Very Expensive ($200,000–$1,000,000)**
$$$$$	**Ridiculously Expensive (more than $1,000,000)**

03: WHAT TO DO: SPACE MISSIONS

Space tourists have a variety of missions to choose from. Whether you're interested in a zero-gravity flight (in which you'll experience the sensation of weightlessness) or a seven-day excursion to the International Space Station, there are vacation packages available for every type of budget and lifestyle.

ZERO-GRAVITY FLIGHT

>> **COST: $**

>> **TRAVEL AND TRAINING TIME: 3–5 DAYS**

>> **MISSION TIME: 1–2 HOURS**

During your zero-gravity flight, you will enjoy the incomparable feeling of weightlessness that astronauts experience while they're in orbit—except your trip will occur within the confines of the Earth's atmosphere in a safe, controlled environment.

Zero-gravity flights take place in an Ilyushin 76 (IL-76 MDK) or a Boeing 727, specially outfitted jet aircraft regularly used to train cosmonauts and astronauts to work in weightlessness. With cabin seats removed and padding added to the interior, the plane offers a huge, open playground for weightless travelers.

After takeoff, the aircraft flies in a parabolic flight pattern: Beginning from a level position, the plane pitches up to approximately 45 degrees, with the nose up and wings level.

As the airplane flies upward, passengers experience about two times their body weight (or "2 Gs"). Suddenly, the engines are powered back, the airplane glides over the top of the arc, and weightlessness begins. As the plane descends, everyone inside the cabin experiences the sensation of "free fall" for about 30 seconds. During this zero-gravity period, you will "float" in the airplane's cabin, with the ability to spin, roll in somersaults, or simply lie peacefully on your stomach or back—in midair.

As the aircraft finishes its downward trajectory, gravity returns and tourists are positioned safely on the plane's padded floor. But the trip is not over: You will experience 10 to 20 additional zero-gravity parabolas, each giving you an additional 30 seconds of float time. You may "swim" the length of the cabin, conduct short scientific experiments, or twist and twirl as you wish.

Zero-gravity flights are an excellent way to experience the adventure of weightlessness; they are recommended for anyone 18 years of age or older and in good health. Occasionally, tourists experience motion sickness during the high-G "acceleration" phase of the flight. Generally, keeping your eyes focused on a fixed object will help to prevent motion sickness, but various medications are also available to mitigate its effects. Your in-flight personal trainer and the onboard physician will offer assistance should you experience any problems.

V THE PARABOLIC FLIGHT PATTERN OF A ZERO-G FLIGHT.

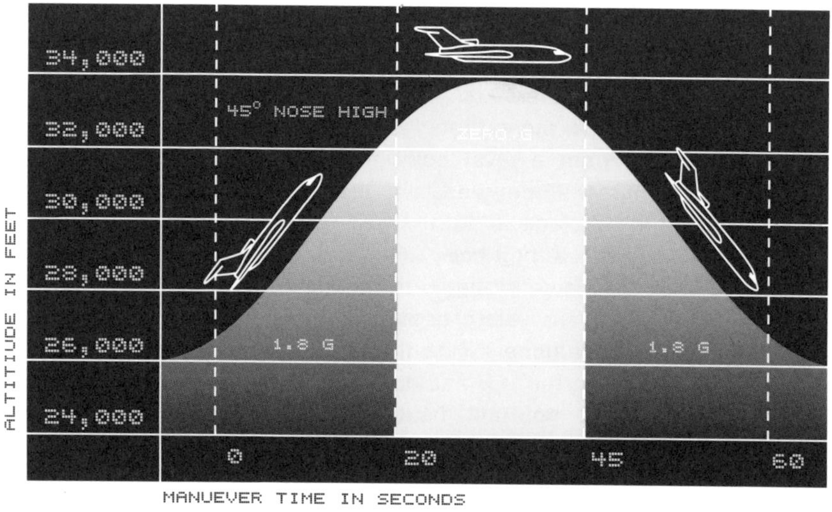

ALTITUDE IN FEET: 34,000; 32,000; 30,000; 28,000; 26,000; 24,000

45° NOSE HIGH

ZERO G

1.8 G

1.8 G

0 20 45 60

MANUEVER TIME IN SECONDS

EDGE-OF-SPACE FLIGHT

>> **COST: $$**

>> **TRAVEL AND TRAINING TIME: 2–3 DAYS**

>> **MISSION TIME: 1 HOUR**

As a tourist visiting the edge of space, you will find yourself higher above the Earth than any human being except the astronauts circling the planet on the International Space Station. At a maximum height of 82,000 feet (25 km), you will see the curvature of the Earth, the deep blackness of space, and a horizon that spans more than 700 miles (1127 km), all from the cockpit of the world's fastest, highest-flying combat jet.

The "edge of space" is the upper edge of the Earth's lower atmosphere and represents the approximate altitude limit of today's conventional jet aircraft. But before reaching "the edge," you will also undergo an experience once only available to professional astronauts: high-gravity training in the world's largest centrifuge.

Due to the immense speed and rocket-like acceleration of your edge-of-space aircraft, the MiG-25 "Foxbat," your training will include a simulation of the high-gravity forces experienced during a rocket launch. To do this, you will ride the TsF-18 Centrifuge, which by high-speed rotation is capable of simulating 30 Gs, or 30 times the force of gravity. (Thirty Gs is beyond human tolerance and is used only for testing equipment.) Because the MiG-25 can travel above Mach 2.5 (two and a half times the speed of sound), you will use the high-G simulator to acclimate yourself to the forces experienced in the plane's cockpit on your way up.

Once airborne on your 30-minute flight, you will be the back-seat passenger as the pilot begins a steep climb nearly straight up. As you pass Mach 1, you will see the MiG's instruments shudder and people on the ground will hear a loud boom: You are now moving faster than the sound of thunder. Nearing 80,000 feet (24.4 km), the jet slows: There isn't enough air for the plane's engines to create additional thrust. From this vantage point, it seems almost as if the plane is floating. Gazing out of the cabin, you see the blackness of space above and the blue and white curve of the Earth below—a view spanning hundreds of miles. Though the temperature outside is about -80°F (-62.2°C), the friction created by your incredible speed makes the glass of the cockpit warm to the touch.

As you descend from the edge of space, your pilot will perform several combat maneuvers, including rolls and dives. Then it may even be your turn. Since this is a training aircraft, you also have a control stick. You might execute a few rolls (with the pilot ready to take over at a moment's notice), after which you would cede control, and the plane would land safely back on Earth. As you gaze up at the sky, you realize you will never look to the heavens in quite the same way again.

SUB-ORBITAL FLIGHT

>> **COST: $$$**

>> **TRAVEL AND TRAINING TIME: 1–2 DAYS**

>> **MISSION TIME: 1–2 HOURS**

Your sub-orbital journey combines the excitement of a rocket-assisted jet flight to orbit with an extended period of weightlessness and a view of Earth. You will undergo extensive training and be outfitted in a spacesuit. And as someone who has visited space, you will be an official astronaut upon completion of your sub-orbital flight.

A sub-orbital flight is a journey that leaves the Earth's atmosphere and enters space but does not reach the speeds required for continuous orbiting of the planet. Though still in the planning phase for space tourists, sub-orbital flight is nearly as old as space flight training itself: Alan Shepard and Virgil "Gus" Grissom achieved sub-orbital flight in 1961, when they became the first two Americans in space.

For space tourists, sub-orbital flight will begin with four days of intensive flight training, including high-G, weightlessness, flight operations and instrumentation, in-flight acceleration, in-flight safety, and equipment training. Before your flight, you will be strapped into your flight chair (possibly while wearing a spacesuit). Flight specialists will discuss safety procedures and go over a final checklist, reviewing everything you have learned over the previous four days.

Your ship will be one of the sub-orbital vehicle systems

currently undergoing development and testing, such as a derivative of *SpaceShipOne*, the C-21, the Rocketplane XP, Xerus (see pages 51–57), or a similarly derived system. Most of these ships will take off using conventional jet engines. At the proper altitude, conventional engines will be shut down, and rocket engines will fire, boosting you to regions above 62 miles (100 km), where space begins.

Once at your maximum altitude, the ship's rocket boosters will shut down. For 5 to 15 minutes, you will be in space: You will be weightless, with a view of much of the Earth, the depths of space, and the Moon. A star map will help you understand the points of light all around you, and crew members will point out the many Earthly points of interest.

Once your space time is complete, the vehicle will descend to the proper altitude and restart the ship's jet engines. You will follow a traditional glide path and land like a conventional aircraft.

The private spacecraft *SpaceShipOne* (see page 51 for a full description) achieved sub-orbital flight on June 21, 2004. Sub-orbital trips for space tourists are likely to be available by 2007 or 2008.

>> VIRGIN GALACTIC

Soon, taking a trip into space will be as easy as flying on an Earth-based airline. In fact, one such airline is already starting to make forays into space tourism: While Sir Richard Branson's Virgin Atlantic has been shuttling passengers around the globe since 1984, sister company Virgin Galactic has announced that it will start offering sub-orbital flights as early as 2008. Their fleet will be based on the X Prize–winning *SpaceShipOne* (see page 51), with maiden ship VSS (Virgin SpaceShip) *Enterprise* almost ready to leap off the drawing boards and into space.

The ship's important systems are expected to be redundant at multiple levels in order to make the VSS *Enterprise* safe enough to carry regularly scheduled space tourists. For fuel, the craft will likely follow the *SS1* design and use nitrous oxide and rubber—both inert until combined—for safer propulsion than that provided by traditional solid and liquid rocket fuel. While of course safety will be a primary concern, this will be one of the first spacecraft designed specifically for passengers, and as such you can expect a more comfortable ride than on a government-operated spacecraft designed for the pros.

Services for astronaut-tourists are still being finalized, but the flight is sure to be unforgettable. You'll start with a six-day training program that could be something like the one described in Chapter 4 (page 85). In addition to medical preparation, simulators, and G-tolerance training, you'll have the chance to speak with experienced astronauts and other space professionals. They'll offer tips for getting the most out of the excitement ahead (including what points in the trip are best for getting those out-of-this-world snapshots).

After a hard day's training, you'll have the chance to relax over a fine meal. Dinner could also be a chance to chitchat with astronauts and even hear guest speakers talk about their experiences in space.

When you're fully trained, it's time to blast off. The VSS *Enterprise* will be carried into the upper reaches of the atmosphere by a mother ship and then released, rocketing into space for a spectacular, crystal-clear view of the stars above and the planet below.

Virgin is now taking reservations for flights through its Web site, www.virgingalactic.com. The expected price is $200,000, with a $20,000 refundable deposit to save a seat. It'll be like no flight you've ever flown before.

SPACE SHUTTLE FLIGHTS

>> **COST:** N/A

>> **TRAVEL AND TRAINING TIME:** N/A

>> **MISSION TIME:** N/A

At the present time, all existing Space Shuttles are owned by the U.S. government and operated by NASA. Though the Space Shuttle Orbiters themselves could conceivably be purchased by private companies for design and research use, sending them into orbit in their present configuration is far too expensive for the private sector.

Instead, the overall design of the shuttles is being studied in the hopes of improving their so-called "piggyback" design, allowing a new generation of spacecraft to enter orbit in similar fashion but at much lower cost. For example, the C-21 spacecraft mimics the orbiter's exterior design, albeit on a much smaller scale, but will likely be launched from a reusable launch vehicle, not from expendable booster rockets.

The shuttle fleet was grounded after the explosion of *Columbia* in February 2003, and the next orbiter mission has been scheduled for sometime in 2005. The use of the Space Shuttle is essential to the completion of the International Space Station, however, and shuttles are expected to begin regular service and supply missions after *Discovery* returns to orbit in 2005.

The Space Shuttle is now nearing the end of its service life, and the program is set to be discontinued in 2010.

In 2004, NASA and President Bush described a vision of the future U.S. space program as one that concentrates on a return trip to the Moon between 2015 and 2020, an eventual manned mission to Mars, and the development of a new manned spacecraft currently known as the "crew exploration vehicle," which will bring astronauts into and out of orbit.

SOYUZ "TAXI" MISSIONS

>> **COST: $$$$$**

>> **TRAVEL AND TRAINING TIME: 4–6 MONTHS**

>> **MISSION TIME: 10–12 DAYS**

Space tourists experience true orbit for an extended period on the ultimate ride, a Soyuz "taxi" mission. On this trip, you will experience a rocket-boosted launch into space, orbital travel in a Soyuz module, docking, life on the International Space Station, and a return trip to Earth in a second Soyuz capsule. Prepare for a week away from home—in a paradise far, far away.

Your taxi mission objective is to resupply the orbiting International Space Station with a new Soyuz capsule and bring the old capsule back to Earth. A Soyuz capsule is attached to the ISS at all times, in case an emergency requires the crew to evacuate the station. Because the in-orbit life of the Soyuz is about six months, the attached capsule is replaced twice a year. This is called a "taxi mission." The total mission time from launch to return is about one week.

Preparation for the taxi mission is intensive: In addition to the standard weightlessness, high-G, and safety training, you will also undergo classroom training; communications, navigation, and electronics training; equipment tests; physical fitness tests; and a psychological review (see the next chapter). All told, expect a six-month program before you take your seat on the Soyuz.

Unlike sub-orbital missions, your taxi mission will depart the Earth using a conventional rocket-propelled launch vehicle, the Soyuz-FG booster. Traveling at thousands of feet per second in your Soyuz-TMA capsule, you will reach orbit in less than 15 minutes. However, it will take your crew approximately two days to maneuver the capsule to the proper speed, altitude, and declination for docking with the ISS.

Though you will not be expected to operate controls or instruments, your crew will keep you apprised of the ship's progress and pertinent mission details. You can expect to be given minor tasks (pushing buttons, taking readings), but for the most part, you will be an observer on this mission. You will have plenty of time for food preparation and picture taking.

After the capsule docks with the ISS, a pressurized hatch will open and you will ask the astronauts on the station permission to come aboard. (Hopefully they'll say yes!) You can expect to be on the ISS for several days as your crewmembers exchange information with the astronauts/cosmonauts on the station. During this period, you will have time to explore the station, conduct experiments, and enjoy the challenges of preparing meals and using the bathroom in a zero-gravity environment (see page 155).

When it's time to leave the ISS, you will enter the descent module of the other docked Soyuz capsule with two crewmembers, detach, deorbit, and reenter the Earth's atmosphere. Though the trip to the station takes two days, reentry spans just a few hours.

POLAR ORBITAL MISSIONS

>> **COST: $$$$$**

>> **TRAVEL AND TRAINING TIME: 4–6 MONTHS**

>> **MISSION TIME: 3–7 DAYS**

A new spaceport in Alaska may present a unique opportunity for space tourists: a chance to orbit the Earth over the North and South Poles. Although these "polar orbital" missions are currently only in the planning stages, the technology necessary to complete such trips is available today.

Currently, most orbital missions launched within the borders of the United States occur from spaceports in Florida or Southern California due to their relative proximity to the equator. A special kind of east–west equatorial orbit, called a "geostationary orbit," is sometimes used for satellites, because such a position allows them to circle the Earth at the equator in 24 hours: The satellites and the Earth move together, in the same direction. Satellites in such orbits appear to remain in a fixed position in the sky.

In polar orbit, objects circle the Earth in a north–south direction, as opposed to the more common east–west orientation. Polar orbit is a 90-degree inclination (or angle) that provides more complete coverage of the Earth's surface. Polar spaceports make reaching such orbits more efficient, because all of the spacecraft's energy can be used for north–south velocity, with little used for east–west velocity.

Future space tourists may launch from the Kodiak Launch Complex at Narrow Cape on Kodiak Island in southern Alaska. Once in orbit, tourists would have spectacular, close-up views not readily available from other orbits: polar ice caps, frozen seas, and towering Antarctic mountain ranges.

TRANS-LUNAR CRUISES

>> **COST: $$$$$**

>> **TRAVEL AND TRAINING TIME: 3–5 DAYS**

>> **MISSION TIME: 7–14 DAYS**

Over the next 20 to 30 years, we will see an increase in commercial space travel, and one destination in particular seems to be especially appealing to entrepreneurs and would-be tourists: the Moon.

Though the technical challenges and costs of building a space station on the Moon are daunting, space enthusiast Robert Bigelow of Bigelow Aerospace envisions a traveling space "hotel" in lunar orbit as the next best thing—and perhaps even an economically feasible idea. Bigelow believes a tourist-supported lunar station could be built for $2 billion and has pledged $500 million of his own fortune to make it a reality.

In 30 years' time, a trans-lunar trip might take a week and cost about $500,000 per tourist (in current dollars). Boarding a private space shuttle, visitors would launch from Earth and rendezvous with the lunar station several days later. In orbit about 10 miles (16 km) above the surface of the Moon, the lunar station would include about 50 staterooms, each with a private bath—and a great view. A slow rotation of the lunar station (imperceptible to guests) would provide about 40 percent of Earth gravity, allowing visitors to "hop" or "long jump" vast distances but avoiding long-term exposure to zero-gravity conditions, which cause a loss of bone density and other health complications. Guests would be shielded from dangerous radiation by glass or clear plastic panels filled with water or liquid hydrogen, which scatter radioactive particles before they harm humans.

The lunar station would be huge by standards of current space structures: 12 times the size of the International Space Station. Bigelow Aerospace estimates that it will take the equivalent of 48 Space Shuttle flights to get the lunar station's building materials into orbit (the station would be primarily aluminum with some structural steel).

Tourists on a trans-lunar mission would undergo several days of basic space training, primarily for high-Gs and weightlessness. However, by the time a lunar space station could become a reality, commercial space flight will have progressed to a point where entering orbit is relatively commonplace.

04: PREPARING YOURSELF: SPACE FLIGHT TRAINING

Space flight offers a range of memorable experiences, from a zero-gravity "float" to divine views of the Earth, solar system, and space. But space is still the "final frontier," and even a quick visit is no walk in the park: Training is required. Although your precise program will depend on the mission you choose, in general any trip to orbit or sub-orbit will require physical fitness training, classroom time, and a detailed medical exam.

THE SPACE FLIGHT MEDICAL EXAM

A week in outer space is slightly more rigorous than a week on a Caribbean cruise. Before you blast off, you will be required to pass a physical to make sure you are a suitable candidate for the high-stress environment of space flight. Although the nature and number of tests—and their duration—will depend on your precise mission and its flight parameters, even short trips on high-performance aircraft will require basic checks of blood pressure and respiration. Longer trips to orbit, during which you will be living in close quarters with your fellow astronauts, require extensive medical and psychological tests.

All space tourists who want to undertake a Soyuz taxi mission to the ISS must pass a rigorous medical examination before traveling into orbit. In addition to the standard check of blood pressure and the monitoring of vital signs, medical personnel may check breathing, vision, and hearing. In some cases, doctors may also request blood work to check enzyme levels, cholesterol, white blood cell count, and other indicators of potentially disqualifying medical conditions.

Depending on existing fitness levels, space tourists should begin training several days to a few weeks before the tests. Jogging, rigorous walking, or other aerobic exercise is recommended to increase endurance, improve heart function, and help the body use oxygen more efficiently. A regular exercise program is an essential part of your preflight training. This program should include cardiovascular and strength training and should be implemented several weeks to a month before your flight. Regular exercise will lead to lower heart rate and blood pressure while at rest and, therefore, to healthier levels during periods of higher exertion.

Additionally, strength training with weights or resistance equipment will increase muscle mass and the strength of tendons and ligaments, improve flexibility and balance, and reduce body fat.

A proper diet is also essential to passing the preflight medical check-up. For several weeks before the exam, avoid sugary foods and those especially high in fat: Such foods may cause weight gain and lead to higher than normal blood pressure. Foods high in protein, such as fish and lean meats, should be combined with leafy green vegetables and moderate helpings of starch. Excess alcohol and caffeine should be avoided; both may cause dehydration. Smoking reduces lung capacity and should be avoided. Junk foods (chips, cookies, candy) contain virtually no nutritional value and should be eaten sparingly or not at all.

>> DISQUALIFYING CONDITIONS

At the present time, any person who is in good overall health may take a space flight. There are a few exceptions, however:

- > Minors (those under 18 years of age)
- > Pregnant women
- > Persons with physical impairments or disabilities that may prevent them from safely evacuating a space station or ejecting from an aircraft
- > Persons with serious heart abnormalities
- > Persons with serious coronary artery disease
- > Persons with diseases affecting major organs
- > Persons with severe vertigo or claustrophobia

>> 30-DAY PREFLIGHT FITNESS SCHEDULE

Thirty days to get in shape? No problem. Here's a diet/fitness plan we recommend:

DAY(S)	ACTIVITY/DURATION	SUGGESTED DIET
1	Light cardio (2 hours walking)	Full breakfast (eggs, dairy); light lunch (salad with grilled chicken); high-protein dinner (steamed salmon with rice)
2–4	Light to moderate cardio (30-minute slow jog followed by 90-minute walk)	Whole-grain pancakes and side of cheese for breakfast; fresh fruit lunch; low-fat protein dinner (pork chops, turkey)
5–14	Morning cardio (45-minute jog or 90-minute bike ride), cool-down period, followed by strength and resistance training every other day	Whole-grain waffles or bagel with cream cheese, hard-boiled egg for breakfast; pasta with meatballs for lunch; dinner of fish with side of broccoli
15–20	Morning cardio (1-hour jog), strength training every other day	Oatmeal, toast, side of cottage cheese for breakfast; salad with grilled tuna for lunch; flank steak dinner (twice per week; trim fat before cooking)
21–26	Morning cardio (1-hour jog or 90-minute bike ride), strength and resistance training every other day	Breakfast of cereal with low-fat milk, toast with cream cheese, fruit; lunch of turkey sandwich with cheese; dinner of lentils with brown rice and salad
27–30	Reduced cardio (30 minutes max per day), strength training on day 27 only	Your choice, but be sensible!

 WEAR PROFESSIONAL ATTIRE AND SIT WITH YOUR BACK STRAIGHT DURING THE MEDICAL EXAM.

HOW TO ACE THE MEDICAL EXAM

Consider the medical examiners the gatekeepers of your trip to space: If they don't pass you, you don't go—no matter how much money you're willing to spend. Though it is of course critical to get a clean bill of health, you must be certain that a personality conflict with an examiner does not lead to your disqualification. No one wants to spend extended periods of time in close quarters with an abrasive, unpleasant, or rude personality.

01: **REMAIN CALM.** A space traveler should not appear to be a nervous person or a person prone to panic or overreaction during stressful conditions. Do not tap your feet, jiggle coins in your pocket, or crack your knuckles: All will make you appear ill at ease.

02: **SIT WITH YOUR BACK STRAIGHT AND YOUR KNEES TOGETHER.** Your posture says much about your attitude and physical condition. You should be straight but not stiff, relaxed but not reclined. Do not slouch. When walking, move with assurance and purpose, keeping your back straight and your hands down by your sides.

03: **ANSWER QUESTIONS CONFIDENTLY AND WITH ASSURANCE.** Remember, you will need to train for this experience, and you will need to be ready for anything. Avoid overconfidence, however. If you do not know the answer to a question, it's better to simply state, "I don't know," than try to bluff your way out and get caught. Look people in the eye when you speak to them, but do not attempt to stare them down.

04: **BE RESPECTFUL.** Your interviewers are professionals and should be treated as such. Address doctors as "Doctor" or "Sir/Ma'am." Do not address medical personnel by their first names unless they specifically ask that you do so. It is appropriate to express disagreement if you feel an error has been made, but do not get angry: Anger will only make you appear defensive, argumentative, and disrespectful of authority—a particularly worrisome trait for a space tourist who will be following orders from crewmembers.

05: **AVOID UNNECESSARY CONVERSATION.** Your preflight examiners are there to do a job. They do not expect excessive casual conversation, nor do they appreciate jokes, long boring stories, or questions about their personal lives. Answer the questions they put to you, but keep your answers brief and to the point. Do not be rude, however. If you sense that the tenor of the exam calls for casual chatting, participate, but do not hog the conversation. Remember that, in general, people would rather talk about themselves than hear you talk about yourself.

06: **DRESS WELL.** Your attire speaks to your professionalism, attention to detail, and self-confidence. Wear a well-pressed suit (for men) or a neat blouse and skirt below the knee (for women). Men should be clean-shaven or have a neatly trimmed beard or mustache. Remove nose rings, eyebrow piercings, and any more than two earrings. Tattoos should be concealed with clothing or make-up. Wear good shoes with a high shine: Remember, these doctors typically interview military personnel and expect neatness.

07: **DON'T BE LATE.** Doctors are busy people, and tardiness is a sign of disrespect and sloppiness. Set two alarm clocks the night before the exam, or get a wake-up call. If you are running late, call ahead and let them know. People tend to get angrier when kept waiting if they are not given an estimated arrival time. (But don't get mad if you have to wait.)

08: **DON'T LINGER.** When the interview is over, thank the doctors for their time and be on your way.

HOW TO SURVIVE THE VESTIBULAR CHAIR

The vestibular chair is used to test the ability of space travelers to concentrate and perform tasks while undergoing the intensive, rotational motion of a spacecraft. The spinning motion of the chair creates imbalances in the inner ear, which cause disorientation and, often, nausea. Trainees will undergo 10 minutes of spinning in the chair, followed by a series of math questions at a desk, under the observation of a psychologist. The math test is followed by 10 additional minutes in the chair.

01: EAT A LIGHT MEAL 60 TO 90 MINUTES BEFORE YOUR "RIDE" IN THE VESTIBULAR CHAIR. You are more likely to experience extreme motion sickness on an empty stomach. Avoid fatty, greasy, and spicy foods: These may cause stomach upset while in the chair. Some experts recommend eating porridge or oatmeal; both foods are relatively easy to regurgitate, if necessary.

02: CLOSE YOUR EYES. Do not attempt to look at a fixed object while in the chair. Focusing will be impossible and will only increase motion sickness.

03: BREATHE DEEPLY AND SLOWLY. By breathing in this manner, you will avoid the risk of hyperventilating.

04: LIMIT MOVEMENT. Excess movement, particularly sharp or extreme moves of your head, will only intensify the effects of the chair. Stay as still as possible, but be sure to follow the instructors' directions if they ask you to move in a particular way (they are likely to ask that you move your head).

05: VISUALIZE YOURSELF IN A SAFE, HAPPY ENVIRONMENT. Do not despair if you quickly become nauseated.

Many space trainees last only a few minutes in the chair before getting sick.

WHILE SEATED IN THE VESTIBULAR CHAIR, TRY TO LIMIT MOVEMENT AS MUCH AS POSSIBLE. V

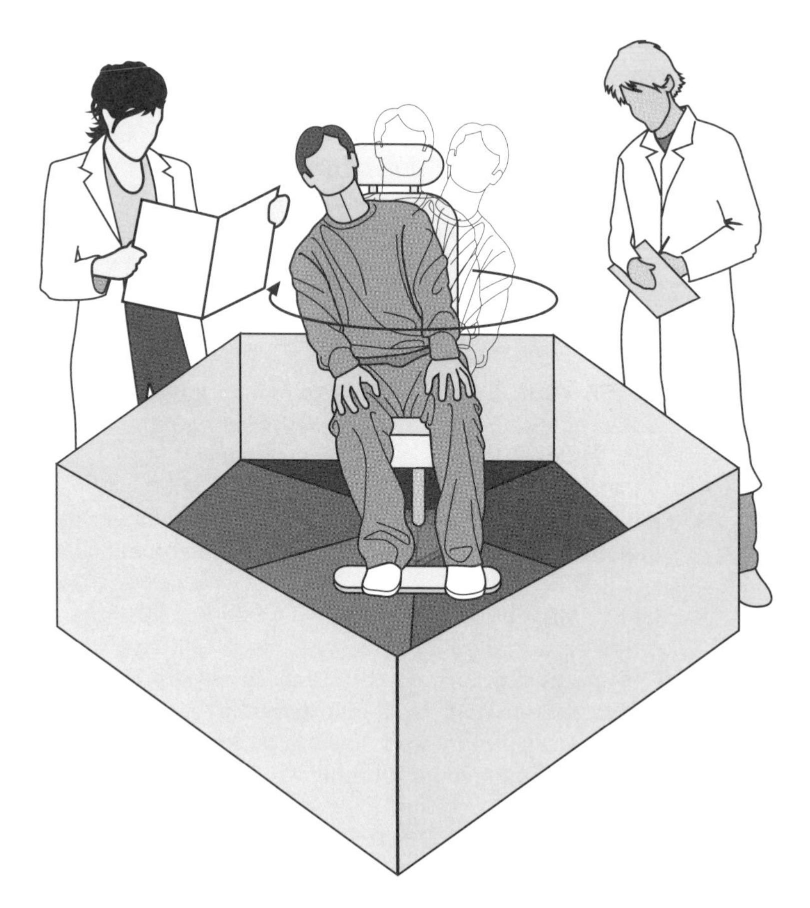

HOW TO APPEAR SANE IN THE PSYCHOLOGICAL EXAM

Before you are allowed to participate in the orbital flight program, you will be given a psychological exam to determine your suitability for space travel. The following tips will help you pass the "psych eval" given to space tourists.

- DO NOT SMILE CONSTANTLY. Your demeanor should be courteous but serious. Smile briefly when first meeting your evaluators, but don't overdo it. Excessive smiling or laughter will indicate nervousness and possible psychological instability.

- DO NOT TWITCH. Twitches and tics are a sure sign that you are not prepared for the high-stress environment of space. Avoid toe-tapping, nail-biting, knuckle-cracking, running fingers through hair, lip-biting, and other indications of impatience or boredom.

- AVOID LOOKING TO THE LEFT WHEN ANSWERING QUESTIONS. People often look to the left when they are lying. Look your evaluator in the eye when replying to questions. Do not stare, however.

- DO NOT MAKE SNAP JUDGMENTS. Think about your answers before vocalizing them. For example, if your evaluators give you a hypothetical emergency to deal with, do not immediately say, "I'd bail out."

- AVOID USE OF THE "ROYAL WE." Do not refer to yourself in the third person or say "we" when you mean "I." Both are indications that you may have control issues or problems dealing with authority figures.

- AVOID UNCONTROLLABLE SOBBING. A crying fit is sure to get you disqualified from the mission.

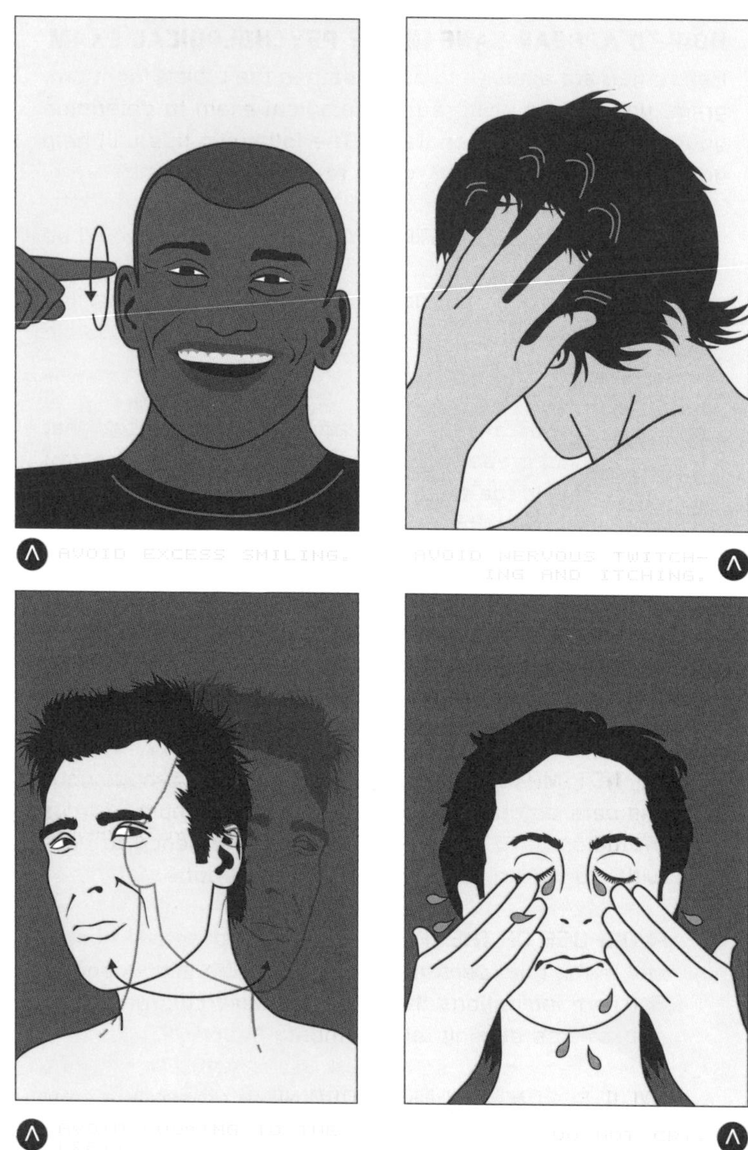

AVOID EXCESS SMILING.

AVOID NERVOUS TWITCHING AND ITCHING.

AVOID LOOKING TO THE LEFT.

DO NOT CRY.

CLASSROOM AND EQUIPMENT TRAINING

If you're planning a space vacation, physical training is only half the battle. You'll also need to bone up on some elementary scientific topics. Here's a crash course.

THEORY OF ASTRODYNAMICS

Though not essential for space tourists, a basic understanding of astrodynamics, or the motion of objects in space, will make your trip more fulfilling—and will help you make sense of the terms you hear during training and space flight. The following explanations should help you get a jump on your classroom instruction.

WHAT IS AN ORBIT?

An orbit is a regular, repeating path one object in space takes around another. An object in orbit is known as a satellite and may be natural or man-made. Orbits are elliptical in shape, and for planets they are usually round (a circle is really just a type of ellipse); comets and some other objects have long "eccentric" or "squashed" orbits. The closest point an orbiting object comes to Earth is known as its "perigee," while the farthest is its "apogee." A low Earth orbit (LEO) is any orbit with perigee and apogee altitudes between 200 and 1,600 miles (322–2,575 km) from the Earth's surface. The Space Shuttle, International Space Station, and space tourism companies all operate in LEO.

WHAT IS GRAVITY?

Gravity is a force of attraction that exists between any two masses, bodies, or particles. Gravity extends from an object in all directions but diminishes with distance. The English physicist Isaac Newton "discovered" gravity in the sense that he first described its effects and created the equation that determines how it acts on objects. Newton's Law of Gravity says that the force of gravity is proportional to the product of the two masses (M and m) and inversely proportional to the square of the distance (r) between their centers of mass. $F = (GMm)r^2$ where G is the gravitational constant: It has a value of $6.6726 \times 10^{-11} m^3 kg^{-1} s^{-2}$.

WHAT IS ESCAPE VELOCITY?

Though it sounds dire, escape velocity is simply the speed at which an object must travel to break free of the planet's gravity and leave its orbit. Escape velocity varies depending on the mass (size) of the planet and the distance of the escaping object from the planet's center. Escape velocity of a rocket from the Earth's surface is approximately 7 miles (11.3 km) per second. "Orbital velocity" is the speed needed for an object to stay in orbit; at an altitude of 150 miles (242 km, or low Earth orbit), orbital velocity is approximately 17,000 miles per hour (27,359 km/h), which is slightly less than full escape velocity.

WHAT IS WEIGHTLESSNESS (MICROGRAVITY)?

Microgravity is a condition in which the sensible effects of gravity are greatly reduced, to an extent that people and objects in such conditions "float" or appear to be weightless. Though microgravity can be simulated on Earth, either with parabolic airplane flights or underwater, continuous microgravity conditions exist only in space.

Even in space, however, microgravity does not represent the absence of gravity: For space travelers to experience one-millionth of Earth's gravity, they would have to be 3.96 million miles (6.37 million km) away, or 17 times farther than the Moon.

Instead, microgravity conditions exist because people, ships, and space stations are in a perpetual state of freefall, while their forward momentum moves them fast enough to overcome the force of gravity. Because objects in freefall experience weightlessness when their acceleration is equal to gravity (approximately 9.8 meters per second squared), objects in orbit create weightlessness by maintaining a constant state of freefall.

TYPES OF ROCKETS AND SPACECRAFT

In the classroom, you will learn about the four major types of rockets and spacecraft used to send space tourists into orbit. Although new vehicles are being developed all the time, even new technologies fall under one of these categories or a combination of two categories.

EXPENDABLE

Expendable rockets are those used primarily for launching unmanned payloads (usually satellites) into orbit. These rockets are based on ballistic missile designs. Most expendable rockets include multiple parts (stages) that separate after they are used; this reduces weight (drag) on the remaining parts. These rockets generally use boosters consisting of an oxidizer combined with rocket fuel.

REUSABLE LAUNCH VEHICLE (RLV)

RLVs are vehicles that can be launched into space and then recovered and used again. The Space Shuttle is considered a semi-RLV: The orbiter and its external solid booster rockets can be reused, but its main external fuel tank cannot. Several types of RLVs are currently under development (see "Horizontally Launched" section).

VERTICALLY LAUNCHED

To date, all government-sponsored manned missions to orbit have used vertically launched spacecraft. With the exception of the Space Shuttle, these craft have been multi-stage, modular systems perched atop booster rockets. One module is generally used for entry into orbit and deorbit, while others are used for navigation and instrumentation and in-orbit propulsion. Vertically launched spacecraft such as the Soyuz have been used to ferry space tourists to the Space Station.

HORIZONTALLY LAUNCHED

Most private space vehicles being built today are horizontally launched spacecraft, among them *SpaceShipOne*, Rocketplane, C-21, and Xerus. Such ships, sometimes called "spaceplanes," take off and land like conventional airplanes (and in fact may use a jet aircraft as a launcher). Horizontally launched vehicles may take off under their own power or may drop from the fuselage of an airplane and then fire booster rockets to reach orbit. Horizontally launched spacecraft are generally considered to be more economical to operate than other types of space vehicles.

LANGUAGE TRAINING

As a space tourist flying on a Soyuz, you will not be expected to be fluent in any language except English. However, you will spend several hours in the classroom learning basic Russian words and pertinent commands. The following chart is a rough guide to the words and phrases you should commit to memory.

ENGLISH	RUSSIAN PHONETIC PRONUNCIATION
Yes	da
No	nyet
Thank you	spa-SEE-buh
Hello	ZDRAS-tvwee-tyeh
Goodbye	dah-svee-DAN-yah
What is our altitude?	Ka-KOH-va NA-sha VIH-suh-tah?
What is our speed?	Ka-KOH-va NA-sha SKOH-rust?
What are we looking at?	Na shto mih SMOH-trim?
What does this button do?	Dlya che-VOH EH-tah KNOHP-ka?
Is it okay to press this now?	MOHZH-nah yeh-YOH NAH-zhut sey-CHAHS?
When should we bail out?	Kahk-DAH min dahlzh-NIG prig-NYOOT spah-rah-SHYOO-tum?
When will this spinning stop?	KAHK-da EH-tuh vrah-SHEY-nyeh ah-stah-NOH-vee-tsuh?
What a beautiful view!	Kah-KOY krah-SEE-vih veed!
Zero-G and I feel fine!	Yah CHOOST-vooyoo she-BYAH khuh-rah-SHO nyeh-veh-SOH-mus-TEE!

COMMUNICATIONS TRAINING

Space tourists will be trained to use the same orbit-to-Earth communications systems used by astronauts. Types of these are as follows.

HAM RADIO

Since 1983, astronauts on the Space Shuttle have used amateur (ham) radio to speak to other radio operators on Earth, particularly educators and school children. The Space Shuttle Amateur Radio Experiment, or SAREX, will allow you to speak to family, friends, and even strangers with access to ham radio equipment.

SOFTPHONE VIA INTERNET PROTOCOL

To make true telephone calls, you will use the "Softphone," a headset connected to a laptop computer. Dialing a number via keypad, you will speak through an attached microphone. As with Internet telephony, voice signals are converted to data "packets" and sent via IP to a satellite, then decoded on Earth. However, because of the distances involved, there will be a lag time (delay) of up to one second; speaking slowly will make the lag more manageable.

Be aware that the Softphone is not always available. Occasionally, the satellite used to transmit signals will be out of range. Signals may also be blocked by the Space Station or scrambled by solar bursts of radiation.

ORBITAL COMMUNICATIONS ADAPTER

This device is used to send e-mail, digital photos, and video to coworkers and family members. This high-speed system is relatively new but has proven highly effective for sending large data files to Earth; it is very popular among astronauts.

SPACESUIT AND EQUIPMENT TRAINING

During your training, you will learn the components of your launch/reentry equipment, which includes a spacesuit with survival systems, communications gear, and various anti-G and pressurization controls.

Because the International Space Station is pressurized, it offers a "shirtsleeve" environment that does not require special suits while in orbit. (Spacewalks require the EMU, or Extravehicular Mobility Unit, which is a pressurized spacesuit with special life support systems; see page 148 for a description.) However, you and your crewmates will wear a special spacesuit during launch and reentry called the Sokol, made by the Russian company Zvezda.

The Sokol SK-1 is a pressurized suit with special features designed to protect space travelers in the event of a fire, evacuation, loss of pressure, or other emergency during launch or reentry. The Sokol has five main functions:

- Protection from loss of oxygen
- Protection from loss of cabin/capsule pressure
- Protection from frigid air and water temperatures
- Protection from extreme heat and flame
- Protection from blood pooling caused by microgravity

Because the Sokol prevents cooling of the body via perspiration, the suit is attached to a portable ventilation unit that pumps cool air into the suit and removes heat from extracted air; astronauts carry the unit with them onto the Soyuz.

The outer layer of the Sokol is a flame-retardant material similar to the fire protection suits worn by race car drivers. The suit is entered via a "V"-type opening in the front, which

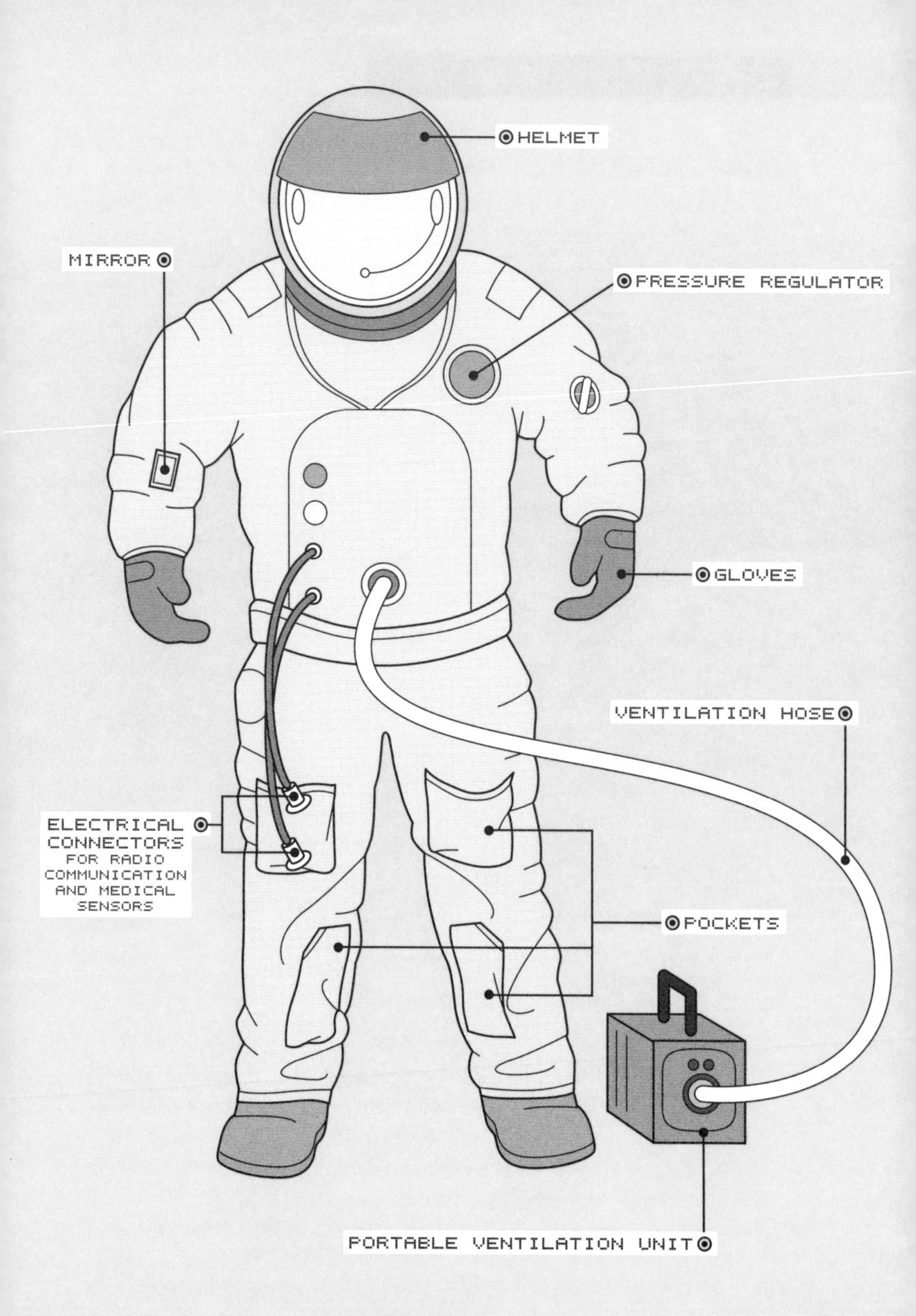
HELMET
MIRROR
PRESSURE REGULATOR
GLOVES
VENTILATION HOSE
ELECTRICAL CONNECTORS FOR RADIO COMMUNICATION AND MEDICAL SENSORS
POCKETS
PORTABLE VENTILATION UNIT

is then sealed with a rubber strip and a zipper. Each suit is custom-made to fit the space traveler and includes a helmet; gloves and boots are separate.

The Sokol is fully insulated against cold temperatures, should crewmembers be forced to evacuate at high altitude or over water. The suit is completely sealed: The air vent has a valve to prevent water from entering, and a neck flange seals the connection between the helmet and the suit itself.

Gloves attach to the suit via two sealable metal flanges. The gloves pressurize with the suit, but have adjustable straps to help regulate internal pressure to make movement of hands and fingers easier. There is a pressure gauge on the left arm of the suit.

The Sokol supports an additional anti-G element, which can be connected to a controller for landing. The anti-G function puts added pressure on the abdomen and the lower body. When connected, the pressure bladders can be controlled by turning a knob.

The Sokol helmet includes an external tinted visor/sunshade which can be lowered by hand. A valve at the rear of the helmet allows ambient air to enter when the visor is closed and no oxygen supply is connected. The helmet contains communications gear, including noise-canceling microphones and padded headphones. Cables connect through the helmet to the spacecraft's communications system.

SPACE STATION SYSTEMS TRAINING

Astronauts are both generalists and specialists. Each crewmember on the Space Station must know enough about each station system to understand how many systems operate, but will specialize in one or two particular systems; specialization requires additional training beyond the general operator level.

As a space tourist, you will not be expected (or allowed)

to perform mission-critical procedures. However, during your training you will receive a briefing on the basic operations of the International Space Station to familiarize yourself with the day-to-day activities in orbit. The ISS has ten primary systems for which crewmembers receive instruction. They are:

- Command and Data Handling
- Communications and Tracking
- Electrical Power
- Environmental Control and Life Support
- Guidance, Navigation, and Control
- Inventory Management
- Operations Local Area Network
- Robotics
- Structures and Mechanisms
- Thermal Control

During your training, you will learn just the basics of the systems you need to operate to make your stay on the station safe and comfortable. You will learn:

- Space Station layout
- Toilet operation (see page 155)

- Operation of communications gear (see page 101)
- Operation of lights and ventilation fans
- Food preparation and drinking techniques
- Warning signals for fire, loss of pressure, and loss of station altitude
- Gas mask and emergency oxygen use

ZERO-G AND H PHYSICAL TRA

Prolonged weightlessness is the most unusual and challenging aspect of space travel; it is also the most fun. Zero G (also called microgravity) makes even the most basic tasks (eating, sleeping, using the bathroom) difficult to master.

High-G environments are less pleasant, but they are an unavoidable part of any space vacation (particularly during launch and your return to Earth). Before entering orbit, you will undergo extensive microgravity and high-G training to help you acclimate to your new environment.

ZERO-G TRAINING: HOW TO MAINTAIN CONTROL IN WEIGHTLESSNESS

This training uses special aircraft that follow parabolic flight patterns. The plane will be traveling at speeds much faster than those of a commercial airliner, you will be climbing and diving at steep angles, and you will "float" for the first time. The following tips will help you prepare for your weightless experience.

01: STAY CALM. It is natural to be scared and nervous in any new environment. However, panic tends to be self-reinforcing and creates additional problems, including muddled thinking, difficulty in solving problems, hyperventilation, and increased heart rate and blood pressure. Remember that you can handle the situation and that there are trainers here to help if you need it.

02: WEAR COMFORTABLE (BUT NOT TOO LOOSE) ATTIRE. Remember: In microgravity, things tend to fly around. Do not wear an open coat or jacket, a dress or skirt,

or accessories (handbags, scarves) that may come loose and cause a problem.

03: **HOLD ON.** At least for your initial zero-G session, do not attempt to float freely or do back flips. Hold tight to the handrail until you become accustomed to the strange sensation of weightlessness. Try to get a sense of how fast or slow your body moves and how much energy is required to move your arms and legs a particular distance.

04: **AVOID MOTION SICKNESS.** It is critical to stay seated (or lie flat) during the ascent ("overload") of your zero-G flight: Most motion sickness occurs during this high-G period. In microgravity, avoid sharp movements of your head to reduce motion sickness. You will be given a special motion sickness bag that looks like a plastic grocery sack: You must use it if you feel you are going to vomit. The in-flight doctor will offer assistance, should you need it.

05: **LISTEN TO YOUR INSTRUCTORS.** It is critical that you pay attention to your zero-G trainers and follow all of their instructions. Do not attempt to move about the aircraft until you are told it is safe to do so. Remember, personnel are here to make sure you enjoy yourself but also to keep you safe.

ZERO-G TRAINING: HOW TO RUN CIRCLES AROUND THE AIRCRAFT

One of the most enjoyable activities during zero-gravity training is running around your aircraft. The fun part is the ability to run up the walls of the cabin, across the ceiling, and down the other side (think Spider-Man). Although executing the run quickly takes practice, the skill itself is not hard to master if you follow these steps.

01: **TAKE SMOOTH, GENTLE STEPS.** Fast motions may send you tumbling head over heels into the center of the cabin. Relax your muscles while you concentrate on each part of your run: cabin wall, ceiling, cabin wall, and floor.

02: **PICTURE YOUR RUN NOT AS A SPRINT, BUT AS A LEISURELY STROLL.** Using minimal pressure, just touch your toes to the sides of the cabin. The pressure you apply should be forward pressure (to propel you forward), not downward pressure (as if you were walking on Earth).

WHEN ATTEMPTING TO WALK UPSIDE DOWN, MOVE SLOWLY UNTIL YOU HAVE MASTERED THE SKILL.

03: **TAKE LONG STRIDES.** As each foot touches and then floats off the wall of the plane, move the other leg slowly forward, taking a long stride before touching down again with the other foot.

04: **USE YOUR HANDS.** Throughout, you may need to use your hands to maintain position. Use a crawling motion while floating, gently touch the ceiling, and then push off until you are comfortable walking upside down. It may take several times before you get the hang of it.

05: **REPEAT.** Once you become proficient, you should be able to walk around the perimeter of the cabin at least twice during each weightless parabola.

HIGH-G/ZERO-G TRAINING: HOW TO PREVENT MOTION SICKNESS

In general, motion sickness occurs during high-G periods, not during microgravity. However, the duration and intensity of motion sickness is highly variable from person to person. The following tips will help you avoid or overcome motion sickness during high-G/zero-G training.

- **EAT, BUT SPARINGLY.** Just before your zero-G training, have a light meal, but make sure not to gorge. You are more likely to become nauseated on an empty or overly full stomach.

- **CLOSE YOUR EYES.** Most experts recommend keeping your eyes closed during the high-G periods of the parabolic flight. Do not try to look around or focus on nearby objects: Both actions may cause you to become disoriented or nauseated.

- STAY STILL. Limiting movement, especially head movement, will reduce motion sickness. The high-G environment also serves to make movement difficult.

- FOCUS. Keep your thoughts on your goal: traveling to space. Realize that this difficult training is all a part of the incomparable joy of space travel.

- KEEP PERSPECTIVE. Though it may seem to be lasting forever, remember that high-G training is just a short part of your overall training regimen. It will all be over soon.

HIGH-G TRAINING: BASIC COMMUNICATION

Astronauts train for years to complete specific mission tasks during periods of high-G loads, particularly launch and de-orbit/reentry into the atmosphere. As a space tourist, you will be expected only to endure, not perform. Nevertheless, you will undergo a physical training course that includes high-G loads, simulated via centrifuge, to prepare.

Speech requires the expansion of muscles in the chest and abdomen. Since these muscles are compressed during periods of high-Gs, normal conversation ranges from difficult to impossible. Follow these steps to make speech easier and more understandable.

- BE BRIEF. Avoid conjunctions, pronouns, and unnecessary adjectives. Do not say, "Could you please stop the machine now? I'd like to get off." Rather, say, "Stop. Now. Want. Off."

- BE CONCISE. Don't force your trainers to decipher complex commands or requests. Don't say, "If this centrifuge were to malfunction, in which direction would my body be propelled?" Ask before the test.

SPEAK IN SHORT BURSTS. Make your point using a single exhalation. Do not attempt to say, "Excuse me (pause, breath). If I could have a moment (pause). I'd like to know when this segment will be over?" Rather, say, "Time left?"

HIGH-G TRAINING: HOW TO ESCAPE AN UNCONTROLLABLE AIRCRAFT

Though it has never happened during a space tourism trip, the slim possibility of a major malfunction on a high-G aircraft always exists. You must be prepared for immediate action should your pilot decide that ejection is necessary. The details below outline the steps necessary to survive a high-altitude, high-G ejection.

01: STAY CALM. Studies have shown that the majority of deaths during ejection have occurred because pilots panic and eject too early, when airspeeds are too high. Although your pilot is likely to eject you (rather than have you eject yourself), it is critical that you stay calm and wait for the ejection command. If you panic and eject too early, you may be killed.

02: LISTEN TO YOUR PILOT. Your pilot is a highly trained, highly skilled aviator who understands aircraft dynamics and proper ejection survival procedures. You, on the other had, may be on your first flight in a high-performance fighter jet. Just because you feel that the aircraft is out of control does not necessarily make it so: Your pilot is likely to be able to recover from most mishaps. Always pay attention to and follow your pilot's instructions.

03: STAY FOCUSED. An ejection command is just that: an imperative to be followed, not questioned. Your pilot will never say, "Eject! Eject! Just kidding . . ." If you hear the word "Eject!" it is only for obeying, not for discussing. If your pilot does not eject you (or directs you to eject yourself), pull the ejection handle; depending on the aircraft and seat manufacturer, the handle will be located between your legs or on the left or right side of the seat. (Your pilot will identify its location before your flight.)

04: **MAINTAIN PROPER POSITION.** Keep hands, arms, and legs in tight to your body when you eject. (Your seat may be equipped with arm and leg clamps that deploy during ejection to assist you.) Many injuries during ejection occur from windblast, which causes severe flailing of appendages and may result in dislocations, fractures, and retinal injuries.

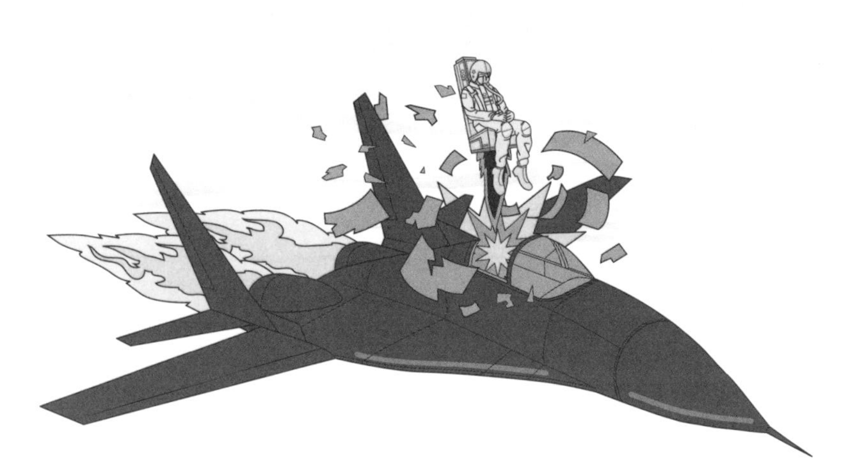

DURING EJECTION, KEEP YOUR ARMS AND LEGS CLOSE TO YOUR BODY.

05: **PREPARE FOR A ROUGH RIDE.** Your seat is actually a small rocket, and when it fires, you will travel up a rail and out of the cockpit at very high speed, with acceleration as high as 20 Gs. Several seconds after ejection, you will feel the very hard tug that accompanies the sudden deceleration caused by drogue parachute deployment, which occurs automatically (hopefully). The drogue chute serves to slow your acceleration before your main parachute is deployed. (The drogue will generally deploy only during high-speed/high-altitude ejections.)

06: **LAND.** Your landing is likely to be fast and hard and may cause ankle, leg, or back injuries. If possible, try to approach the ground from a slight angle, not from directly above, and roll onto your shoulder as soon as your feet touch down.

HIGH-G TRAINING: THE TsF-18 CENTRIFUGE

The centrifuge is used for simulating both high-G enviroments and physiological weightlessness. The world's largest centrifuge, the TsF-18 in Star City, Russia, can generate up to 10 times the force of gravity for manned training and up to 30 times for unmanned experimentation. During the simulation, you will experience the following:

- SOYUZ LAUNCH THROUGH INSERTION INTO EARTH ORBIT: Maximum 4 G, duration 9 minutes
- ORBITAL FLIGHT: Weightlessness simulation, duration 60 minutes
- SPACECRAFT DEORBITING AND REENTRY: Maximum 6.5 G, duration 7 minutes

THE CENTRIFUGE IS AN ENORMOUS "RIDE" DESIGNED TO REPLICATE HIGH-G CONDITIONS.

First, you will be dressed in a jumpsuit with attached sensors that monitor your heart rate, breathing, and other vital signs. Next, you will be placed in the "cockpit," actually the TsF-18's cabin, where you will be seated in front of a video camera used for observation. A speaker and microphone are used for giving instructions and two-way communication. The technicians will tell you when you move to new segments of the launch simulation.

01: **EAT LIGHTLY.** A small meal is recommended an hour or two before your "ride" on the centrifuge.

02: **RELAX.** Because there is little you can do to physically prepare your body for the unfamiliar sensation of high Gs, mental preparation is key. Try to relax. Keep your limbs loose, and try to find a comfortable position in the cabin's seat.

03: **ACKNOWLEDGE YOUR FEARS.** Brave people are not fearless. Rather, they acknowledge their fears and seek ways to overcome them. Do not be afraid to tell yourself (and the technicians) that you are feeling nervous or apprehensive. Fear is a natural reaction to the unknown, and nothing to be ashamed of. Remember, you are a space tourist, not an astronaut with years of training.

04: **BREATHE.** Breathing during high-Gs will be labored and difficult. To reduce nausea, try to breathe from your abdomen, not your chest. If you hold your breath, you will pass out more quickly; though this may seem preferable to being conscious in the spinning centrifuge, it will only serve to make you repeat the failed segment.

05: **KNOW THAT YOU ARE IN CONTROL.** It is helpful to realize that you have the ability to stop the TsF-18 at any time: During the simulation, you will hold down a button on the "dead man's stick." If you cannot take the G forces any longer, release the button to stop the centrifuge.

Though not precisely the same as a centrifuge, a very tall, very fast roller coaster can simulate higher-than-normal G-loads. If time permits, take several rides on such 'coasters to better acclimate yourself to the physical sensations of high gravity.

05: SPACE TRAVEL

Finally, after weeks (or months) of preparation, the big day has arrived. You're in top physical shape (or as close as you're likely to get), your training is complete, and you've passed the preflight exams. Now comes the fun part.

LAUNCH

Launch is without question the most exciting part of your space journey—and the process begins long before the rockets start firing. Here's everything you need to know to get off the ground.

QUARANTINE: WHY IT'S NECESSARY

For one to two weeks before your orbital space flight, you will be placed into monitored quarantine at the launch facility's astronaut quarters. This means:

- You will not be allowed to touch or come into the physical proximity of others.
- You will not be allowed to leave the launch facility at any time or for any reason.
- You will be permitted to eat and drink only substances approved by flight surgeons.
- Your sleep and wake-up schedule will be determined and supervised by the preflight crew training team.

Disregard for prelaunch quarantine rules may (and likely will) disqualify you from space flight. There are several good reasons for the quarantine period, including:

- To make sure you have not caught and will not catch a cold, the flu, or another contagious sickness that may cause others in your spacecraft or on the International Space Station to become ill.

- To prevent you from missing or being late for the scheduled launch.
- To prevent you from being too intoxicated to launch.
- To protect you from an accident, kidnapping, or other situation that may delay or scrap the launch.

QUARANTINE DOS AND DON'TS

Quarantine can be monotonous and boring and offers lots of time for you to develop apprehension about your upcoming trip. These tips will keep you focused on your exciting journey and help the time pass quickly.

DO:

- Exercise for two hours daily. This will help you sleep well and minimize nervousness or anxiety.
- Talk to your crew about why you have chosen to go to space, what you expect to feel during your flight, and what you'll do after you're back on Earth.
- Write letters to your friends and family, to be sent after you launch.

DON'T:

- Attempt to sneak any alcohol or other controlled substances into the quarantine area. You will be caught, and your trip will be canceled.
- Play pranks or practical jokes on your crew. General

good humor is expected, especially when you are cooped up together for long periods. More serious pranks and scares, however, will not be appreciated during this period of nervousness and preflight jitters. Such behavior will also serve to alienate you from the rest of the crew and make you feel like an outsider. Avoid telling off-color jokes that might offend.

Worry about your space flight. You are trained, healthy, and prepared for any eventuality. Try to relax and enjoy the moment.

YOUR PERSONAL ITEMS: WHAT YOU CAN BRING

Transporting things to and from space is very costly, so expect restrictions on the number of personal items you are allowed to bring. On a short sub-orbital flight, you'll be limited to a handful of carry-on items; on an orbital flight with a weeklong stay at a space station, you'll be limited to about 22 pounds (10 kg) of luggage—the equivalent of a small suitcase.

The items you'll probably want to bring will fall under four basic categories.

MISSION IMPLEMENTATION ITEMS: These include experiments, data recorders, materials samples, or anything you need to complete your mission in space (this is assuming, of course, that you *want* a mission—many tourists will be happy to sit back, relax, and enjoy the view).

PERSONAL RECORDING AND MEDIA EQUIPMENT: You should bring the highest-quality and lightest digital camera, camcorder, voice recorder, and other electronics that you can afford. This may be your only trip to space, and you'll want to capture as much of the experience as you can.

SOUVENIRS: Bring small items that you can give to friends and family members upon your return to Earth. Coins, pins, cloth badges, stamps, and stickers make excellent keepsakes—who wouldn't want a nickel that's orbited the Earth? Plus, these items are all lightweight, and they won't take up a lot of room in your suitcase.

OTHER PERSONAL ITEMS: For the trip into orbit, you will not have to worry about personal hygiene items, food, water, or other necessities. These will be provided for you and will not be included in your weight allotment. In addition, to reduce cargo weight, astronauts generally change clothes (pants and T-shirts) only once every few days. However, it's still considered normal to change your underwear daily.

CARGO CHECKLIST

Consider bringing the following items on your space vacation:

- Digital camera (with as many megapixels as available) and at least one telephoto lens
- Digital camcorder (preferably one that writes directly to DVDs)
- Several blank DVDs and 1-gigabyte memory cards
- Lightweight digital voice recorder for recording your thoughts. (In space, you'll need to learn how to hold a pencil all over again; recording your thoughts by voice is much easier.)
- Small MP3 player with 20–30 hours of your favorite music
- Small, very lightweight laptop computer for downloading digital photos, sending and receiving e-mail, and other tasks
- 100–200 customized mission pin souvenirs
- 2–3 pieces of lightweight jewelry for your spouse or your closest friends
- Lightweight PDA with calculator and world atlas software (to help you determine what you're seeing from space). Alternatively, bring a small paperback world atlas and a pocket calculator.
- 2–3 science or fun experiments you can perform while in space
- Clean underwear for every day of your trip
- 1 change of clothes for every three or four days in space

T-MINUS ZERO: SECURING YOURSELF IN THE SPACECRAFT

The launch team and your crew will help you prepare for launch. However, you should double-check your seating position and communications gear and check your immediate surroundings to make sure there are no items that might come loose during flight.

01: **ASSUME THE POSITION.** Your custom-fitted seat liner, which will be snug, will keep you in a fetal position: arms in front of you, legs bent at the knee and close to your chest. This position will not be especially comfortable, but your training will have included practice sessions. Because of the potential for discomfort (as well as more severe conditions like blood clots), Mission Control will not allow you to remain in launch position for more than 20 to 30 minutes.

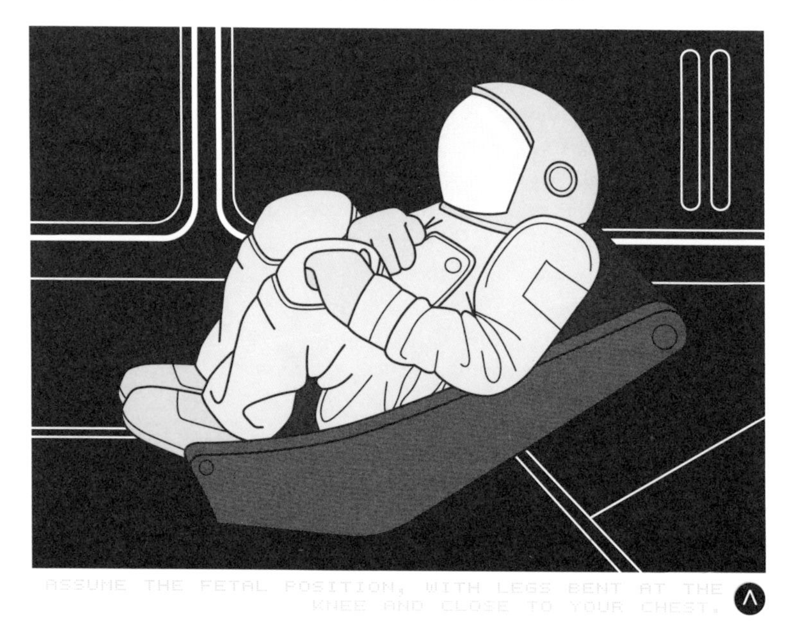

ASSUME THE FETAL POSITION, WITH LEGS BENT AT THE KNEE AND CLOSE TO YOUR CHEST.

02: **FASTEN YOUR SEAT BELT(S).** You will be held in place by a five-point harness system that limits your movement. Make sure all belts are pulled tight and buckles fully closed.

03: **TEST YOUR COMMUNICATIONS SYSTEMS.** Between your legs and within reach of your hands will be a vertical handle; this is the controller for your microphone: Press the button to talk, release to listen. There will also be a small joystick that you will use to change information screens on your monitor. Mission Control will contact you via the system before launch, to ensure that everything is functioning properly.

04: **EXAMINE YOUR SUIT CAREFULLY FOR ANY SIGNS OF RIPPING OR TEARING.** Your helmet should be connected to the neck ring of your spacesuit. Move your sun visor to the down position.

05: **AWAIT YOUR INSTRUCTIONS.** Mission Control will review everything you need to do, and it's your job to follow these instructions to the letter. Listen closely and don't deviate from the plan.

CELESTIAL NAVIGATION

Travel on earth is relatively two-dimensional: At any given moment, you're either heading north or south, east or west. Space adds a third dimension and infinite complications. Here's everything you'll need to find your way.

HOW TO FIND YOUR BEARINGS IN SPACE

Orbiting through space means continuous motion, with no physical contact with any other object. Finding your bearings can be a challenge. Use these tips to help you understand where you are headed, and where you have been.

- WHAT STARS CAN YOU SEE? You'll learn the basics of celestial navigation through planetarium simulations during your classroom training. But everything you learned as a Boy (or Girl) Scout still applies: The Big Dipper points north, to Polaris (the North Star).

- WHAT DOES THE EARTH LOOK LIKE? Most spacecraft orbit from west to east. Look at the clouds below you. Are they moving toward you or away from you? If things are moving toward you, you are facing east; if away, you are facing west.

- IS IT DAY OR NIGHT? At night, it will be difficult to see details on the Earth's surface. During the day, stars will not be very visible. Luckily, because of your orbital velocity—thousands of miles per hour—night and day last just 45 minutes each. If you are having trouble getting your bearings using one of the methods above, wait about an hour and try the other methods.

CALCULATING YOUR ORBITAL ALTITUDE

How high can you go? In a circular Earth orbit, altitude is always a function of speed. To determine your altitude, all you need to know is your velocity in kilometers per second—information that your crewmates should be happy to provide. Then key the following equation into your PDA or calculator: Altitude = $\mu/(V^2) - R_E$.

Remember that μ is a constant of 3.986×10^8, V is your velocity (expressed in kilometers per second), and R is the radius of the Earth in kilometers, a constant of 6,378. Thus, if you are traveling at 6.0 kilometers per second, your altitude is 4,694 kilometers above the surface of the Earth.

GUIDING YOUR SPACECRAFT TO A SPACE STATION

Guiding a Space Shuttle or Soyuz spacecraft to the Space Station requires precise timing, supremely accurate measurements, and skillful rocket firings. The basic approach, however, is relatively straightforward. As a tourist, of course, you will be strictly observing (Mission Control and your crew will handle the actual maneuvers). But docking will be more enjoyable (and less disconcerting) if you understand each step as it happens.

01: APPROACH THE SPACE STATION FROM THE REAR. The chase begins from a point directly behind and below the target. This trajectory is achieved by waiting for the Earth's rotation to carry you under the "hula hoop" orbit path of the target. At the proper moment—called the "launch window"—you blast off in the same direction the Space Station is moving.

02: TAKE THE "INSIDE TRACK." After launch, your spacecraft is in a lower, faster orbit (akin to the inside track of a racing circuit) but several thousand miles behind the target. Each spin around the Earth (a single orbit) takes about 90 minutes to complete the 25,000-mile (40,233 km) journey.

03: **FIRE THRUSTERS TO ASCEND.** Firing steering rockets (or thrusters) raises your orbit, which causes your speed to drop and thereby slows your approach rate to the Space Station. Mission Control uses a general rule of thumb that says you will approach your target at a rate 10 times your vertical separation of each orbit. For example, if your spacecraft's orbit is 50 miles (80.4 km) lower, you get 500 miles (804 km) closer about every 90 minutes.

04: **ADJUST APPROACH RATE.** In order to arrive at the Space Station at the desired time and with the correct sunlight conditions, your approach rate will be adjusted carefully. To accomplish this complex task, radar on Earth accurately measures your exact flight path, and computers then predict when you would arrive at your target and what changes you need to make in order to stay on course and on schedule. This process can take many hours (up to a full day), which is why it is critically important to "creep up" from behind while these measurements are made. Overshoot the Space Station and your journey will be prolonged by as many as one or two days; it could take that much time to lower your orbit and attempt another rendezvous.

05: **ENGAGE RADAR TO GAUGE YOUR POSITION.** Several hours before your scheduled contact with the Space Station, your spacecraft's radar unit will begin sending signals toward the target. A radar echo generator on the Space Station bounces the signals back, giving precise measurements of the relative position and motion between you.

06: SLOW APPROACH. As the scheduled docking time approaches, your orbit will be raised slightly to trim approach speed, and the ship may now make a few left–right corrections to put you precisely into the target's flight path and within sight of the Space Station. The final step, docking, is described in the next section.

HOW TO DOCK A SPACECRAFT TO A SPACE STATION

Once you have come within sight of the International Space Station, the meticulous work of docking two huge spacecraft in orbit begins. Again, most of the process is computer controlled and automated, though last-minute changes and adjustments will be performed by your crew (and, should a crew member become incapacitated, you may be asked to lend a hand).

01: FIRE THRUSTERS. Approaching from behind and below, small steering rockets begin firing frequently while you and the crew constantly monitor your distance gauge.

02: CEASE FORWARD MOMENTUM. At a range of about 400 feet (122 m), forward movement will stop so you can find a "parking space" on the station. With the Space Station directly in front of you, your speeds must be matched precisely or you risk overshooting or colliding with your target. (In 1997, a cargo vessel collided with the Mir space station, causing major damage, including oxygen loss and temporary spinning of the station.)

03: **LOCATE THE DOCKING PORT.** The Space Station has a specialized docking port used to connect to supply ships, but it is rarely visible from the front of an approaching spaceship. Creeping slowly sideways, you will circumnavigate the station until the docking port is directly in front of you.

04: **RESUME APPROACH.** With the docking port in view, a few short thruster bursts will allow you to resume your approach. You should constantly check the location and position of your target in a monitor until you receive confirmation that the spaceship's spring-mounted probe has slipped into a "docking cone" and latched to its apex.

05: **PREPARE TO MEET YOUR HOSTS.** Welcome to the International Space Station! System thrusters should be turned off before you shake hands with the crew, congratulating them on another successful docking. Someone will show you to your quarters, but don't expect any help with your bags. Out in space, even visitors are expected to carry their own load.

>> SPACE FLIGHT SPECIAL MANEUVERS

Every space flight has its share of complications, so it's best to expect the unexpected. Your crew might need to perform one of these special maneuvers en route to your destination.

FREE RETURN

A spacecraft low on fuel or experiencing a malfunction can return to Earth using "free return," an energy-efficient method of space travel. A free-return orbit allows a spacecraft to change direction by using the gravitational field of a nearby planet or other celestial body. For example, consider a spacecraft en route to the Moon that suddenly needs to return to Earth. Rather than firing its engines to alter course, the spacecraft would use the gravity of the Moon. All the spacecraft needs to do is continue on to the Moon and pass around its far side. As the spacecraft passes by the Moon, lunar gravity will capture the spacecraft and "fling" it back toward the Earth. (A free-return maneuver was used to bring the damaged *Apollo 13* spacecraft back to Earth in 1970.)

GRAVITY ASSIST

Gravity assist is a special maneuver often used to reorient spacecraft that have drifted off course. It can also be used for a craft low on fuel or unable to reach proper orbit.

All planets orbiting the Sun or another celestial body have stored forward speed or angular momentum that can be transferred to a spacecraft through the force of the planet's gravity. To capture this "free" energy, a spacecraft must make a close pass by a planet.

The spacecraft will initially approach the planet's orbit from behind and make a pass close to the body. As the ship enters the gravitational field of the planet, the force of the attraction will impart the planet's angular momentum, accelerating the spacecraft. This energy transfer is much like a spinning skater grabbing on to and flinging a smaller, passing skater. The ship's velocity is "assisted" by the planet's gravity, and the vehicle gains momentum. At this point, as long as the spacecraft's increased velocity is greater than the planet's escape velocity (see "What Is Escape Velocity?", page 97), the ship will pull away from the planet and continue on its assigned orbit.

SPACE EMERGENCIES

A visit to space is not like a visit to Space Mountain. Danger lurks in every corner of the galaxy, and every trip features its share of risks. To many tourists, this risk is part of the appeal. The following guidelines will help you survive some of the worst catastrophes that outer space has to offer.

HOW TO SURVIVE IF YOUR VEHICLE DETONATES ON THE LAUNCH PAD

Your Soyuz spacecraft is equipped with a special escape mechanism should a catastrophic failure cause the explosion of your booster rocket during the launch sequence. This mechanism should function automatically, propelling you to a safe distance.

01: STAY CALM. If your spacecraft's launch escape system has not engaged automatically, your pilot will initiate manual crew capsule detach and escape procedures. Do not panic: Specific procedures are in place in the event of just such an emergency.

02: PREPARE FOR ESCAPE ROCKET FIRING. The upper section of the Soyuz-TMA rocket (the section that contains your spacecraft) will automatically detach from the booster. This is accomplished by the firing of the tractor escape rocket, a powerful rocket with several nozzles. You will feel the rocket fire, and then the separation of the spacecraft from the booster will lift you to safety in a split second.

03: BRACE YOURSELF FOR HIGH GS. After separation from the booster, the escape rocket will propel your spacecraft and its faring (cover) at extremely high speed away from the launch pad to an altitude of several miles. You may experience G forces greater than an actual launch. Tense your body and prepare from labored breathing (see "High-G Training," page 115).

04: PREPARE FOR CAPSULE SEPARATION. Several seconds after detaching from the booster, fins drop down to stabilize the spacecraft and the faring is released into the atmosphere. You will then feel several sharp clunks as the Soyuz capsule's service and orbital modules are ejected.

05: PREPARE FOR CHUTE DEPLOYMENT. After all modules are separated, the main parachute deploys from your ascent/descent module. You will feel a very sharp tug, followed by rapid deceleration as you slow and then drift back to Earth.

06: EVACUATE MODULE. Once back on Earth, follow the instructions of your crewmates with regard to evacuating the module. Keep in mind your escape trajectory may have resulted in a water landing, a potentially dangerous and undesirable situation (see page 173).

HOW TO SURVIVE IF YOU'RE A BYSTANDER

You may request (or be asked) to watch a rocket launch from a viewing area, as a bystander. In general, this activity is perfectly safe, provided you take the proper precautions. However, there is always a slight risk of on-launch explosion, and such explosions have injured or killed bystanders in the past. (In the early and mid-1990s, several Chinese

Long March rockets exploded just after liftoff, killing dozens on the ground.) Take the following steps to increase your chances of surviving a mishap on the launch pad.

01: **LOCATE THE BLAST TRENCH.** There will be one or more deep trenches within several hundred meters of the launch pad. This "blast trench" is designed to protect bystanders in the event of an on-launch explosion. Stand at the very edge of the trench, and be ready to dive in at a second's notice. They are usually about 10 feet (3 m) deep.

02: **WATCH FOR WARNING SIGNS.** A normal launch will include copious amounts of smoke and flame. Be sure these flames are coming from the bottom and aiming downward. If you see flames coming from the side of the booster rocket, or notice flaming pieces of metal shearing away from the booster, be ready to take evasive action.

03: **KNOW WHEN TO RUN.** You will be able to see the explosion before you hear and feel the blast wave. You will have no more than 2 to 3 seconds to act before the blast wave reaches you.

04: **DIVE INTO THE BLAST TRENCH.** Curl into a ball, tuck your head into your body, and cover your ears with your hands. Stay as close to the leading edge of the trench (the edge closest to the launch pad) as possible.

>> FROM MISSION CONTROL

If you cannot reach the blast trench in time, you may be carried tens or even hundreds of yards by the blast wave. If you feel yourself being "picked up," relax and let your body go limp. Do not try to outrun the explosion.

05: IF YOU SEE OR FEEL FLAMES ON YOUR BODY, ROLL ON THE GROUND TO EXTINGUISH FLAMING CLOTHING. Although rocket fuel is extremely flammable, most fuels are not toxic and should not cause injury after initial combustion has passed.

IF YOU WITNESS A VEHICLE EXPLODE, RUN TOWARD THE NEAREST BLAST TRENCH.

HOW TO STABILIZE A SPINNING SPACECRAFT

A thruster malfunction will cause your spacecraft to spin rapidly out of control until steps are taken to resolve the problem. In general, spinning of the spacecraft is caused by a thruster that goes out while the others are still firing. Your crew will follow these steps to restore proper attitude and rotation. Use them as a guide to the process as it happens.

01: CREW WILL TURN OFF ALL THRUSTERS AND CHECK GYROSCOPES. The spacecraft will continue to spin. Because there is no air friction in space, a moving object will continue to move until an equal and opposite force counteracts it. For this reason, you cannot simply begin firing random thrusters in the hopes of counteracting the rotation, as if you were braking a car: You must determine the exact angular velocity and direction of the spinning craft. Gyroscopes provide the crew with this information.

02: ALERT MISSION CONTROL. Once the spacecraft's angle and rate of movement have been determined, these values should be provided to Mission Control. Computers on the ground will determine the precise order and timing for your thrusters to be refired, and this information will be relayed to the crew.

03: REFIRE THRUSTERS. Using the proper firing procedure, the spin can be slowed and the ship reverted to a stable state.

HOW TO DEAL WITH FIGHTS ON THE SPACE STATION

Space can be a stressful environment, and the Space Station's close quarters can exacerbate personality differences and lead to conflict. Fortunately, the microgravity environment limits the amount of physical "fighting" that can occur. The following tips will help you avoid a fight and deal with disagreements in space.

MAINTAIN PROPER "FLOAT" ETIQUETTE. In microgravity, ordinary actions become difficult and minor slips can be highly annoying. If another crewmember is eating, keep your feet away from him/her if you are floating in the same area. Expect a gentle push if you float too close; this is normal and should not cause offense. Similarly, if you are floating and are approaching a crewmate too quickly, grab a handle on the wall to slow your momentum to avoid a collision.

REMEMBER: YOU'RE A GUEST OF THE STATION. As a space tourist, you will be on the station only a short time. Your crewmates, however, may be in orbit for

IF A CREWMEMBER FLOATS TOO CLOSE, GIVE HIM A GENTLE PUSH.

weeks or months at a stretch. Remember that you are the guest here and as such should take pains to be accommodating and respectful of others.

- FOLLOW SPACE ETIQUETTE. Don't force your crewmates to clean up after you. Pay special attention to cleaning the vacuum toilet after use and stowing your dirty meal tray properly.

- DO NOT PLAY CHESS. Though especially popular with Russian cosmonauts, playing chess on the Space Station is serious business and can lead to conflict. Politely decline any invitation to play.

- COOL OFF. If you feel tempers rising, it is best to put physical space between you and your crewmate. Float to opposite ends of the Space Station, or enter the attached Soyuz for a time out.

- APOLOGIZE. The Space Station is a confined area, and two angry crewmates cannot avoid each other for very long. Apologize at your first opportunity and accept blame, even if it's not your fault.

HOW TO EXTINGUISH A FIRE ON A SPACE STATION

A fire in orbit is a very serious condition: Station oxygen is quickly consumed, smoke and toxic particles are released into the air, and a breach of the station's sealed environment can cause catastrophic structural failure. Fortunately, there are simple and specific procedures to follow in the event of fire, as outlined below. You should be ready to help, if asked.

01: LISTEN FOR WARNING SIGNS. A manually triggered fire alarm is a low-pitched warble, while an automated smoke alarm is a warble between high pitches and low pitches. A low-pitched warble means that another crewmember has noted the emergency and is already taking the necessary measures. If you hear an automated alarm, alert the nearest crewmember and stand by to assist if necessary. Of course, if you ever see or smell smoke or flames, you should activate the nearest fire alarm immediately.

02: GATHER YOUR GEAR. Ask the nearest crewmember to help assemble gear. You'll need a protective hazard suit (or at least protective gloves), a gas mask, a flashlight, and a fire extinguisher. The fire extinguisher should be used only in the affected module.

03: FIND AND ASSESS THE FIRE. Remove any nearby electrical equipment, if possible. Using the air-sampling equipment in the emergency kit, take atmospheric readings and note results. If smoke or flames persist, or if the concentrations of the contaminants exceed those in the table shown here, don your hazard suit.

CONTAMINANT	CONCENTRATION
carbon monoxide (CO)	200 parts per million
hydrochloric acid (HCl)	10 parts per million
hydrogen cyanide (HCN)	5 parts per million

04: REPORT TO MISSION CONTROL. Give your situation, fire location, and any available atmospheric readings.

05: **EXTINGUISH THE FLAMES.** Don your gas mask. Using the fire extinguisher, attempt to put out the fire. Note that extinguisher and nozzle temperatures drop far below 32°F (0°C), so use the gloves to protect your hands.

06: **EXAMINE THE FIRE SOURCE.** Check to see if the fire has been extinguished. If it has, take additional necessary atmospheric and air quality readings, assess damage, and report your findings to Mission Control. Otherwise . . .

>> FROM MISSION CONTROL

In microgravity, fire—along with everything else—floats. If you see a floating "fireball" or a piece of flaming metal drifting toward you, quickly soak a blanket in water and attempt to surround and smother the flame, or use a fire extinguisher to put it out.

07: **EVACUATE TO SOYUZ.** If the fire persists (and is not in the Soyuz escape module), move to the Soyuz, close the hatch, and contact Mission Control for further instructions. If the fire is in the Soyuz and cannot be extinguished, don your gas mask and hazard suit, enter with a flashlight, and transfer spacesuits, seat liners, and personal items to the station. Close the hatch and contact Mission Control.

06: LIFE IN SPACE

At last! You've passed your training. You've survived the launch. You've reached the destination of your choice. Now it's time to simply live a little—this is supposed to be a vacation, remember? Even the most routine daily chores take on a whole new meaning when performed outside the Earth's atmosphere. In this next chapter, we'll look at the ins and outs of life in outer space.

ENJOYING SPACE FLIGHT

A trip to orbit offers a wealth of activities that most people will never experience; you are one of the lucky few who will. You will see the entire planet from space, watch cloud formations and storms move across the globe, watch the Sun rise and set every hour, get a close-up view of the Moon, and, of course, experience weightlessness. Though some of these activities require no special skills, others will be much more enjoyable with a few pieces of critical information to guide you.

FINDING AND PHOTOGRAPHING THE BEST VIEWS OF EARTH

Naturally, there's a lot to see in space—but it helps to know what to look for. Because day turns to night (and vice versa) every 45 minutes—with a few minutes of dawn and dusk during each cycle—you'll have plenty of time to spot these landmarks from orbit. Look for the following:

- THE GREAT WALL OF CHINA. One of several man-made object visible from space with the naked eye.
- MT. EVEREST. On a clear day, you can see the mountain's summit easily.
- THE AMAZON RIVER.
- THE BAHAMAS. Astronauts claim the waters of the Bahamas have the most spectacular shade of blue visible from space.

- **HURRICANES.** Hurricane season in the Atlantic runs from June through November; in the eastern Pacific it is mid-May through November. Large storms are easily visible from space.
- **VOLCANIC ERUPTIONS.**
- **LIGHTNING STORMS.**
- **AURORA BOREALIS.**

When shooting still photographs of Earth from the ISS, it is important to remember that the station is moving at nearly 5 miles (8 km) per second, which tends to blur photos at normal shutter speeds. U.S. astronaut Ed Lu, who spent six months on the Space Station in 2003, used a 35mm digital camera for his snapshots but added 50mm and 180mm lenses for wide shots. For photographs of smaller objects, where the field of view was about 10 ground miles (16 km), he used an 800mm lens with a shutter speed of one-800th of a second. Tracking the camera generally creates photos with better resolution, according to Lu.

HOW TO SLEEP IN WEIGHTLESSNESS

Sleeping in space can be a challenge, and not only because of the microgravity. With your spacecraft orbiting the Earth every 90 minutes, the ship is never in complete darkness for very long, which can disrupt the body's natural circadian rhythms. In addition, many astronauts elect to sleep in shifts, so lights may remain on and crewmembers will be working while you are trying to sleep. Some space travelers have also reported disrupted sleep patterns due to motion sickness and the warming rays of the Sun entering the station or ship.

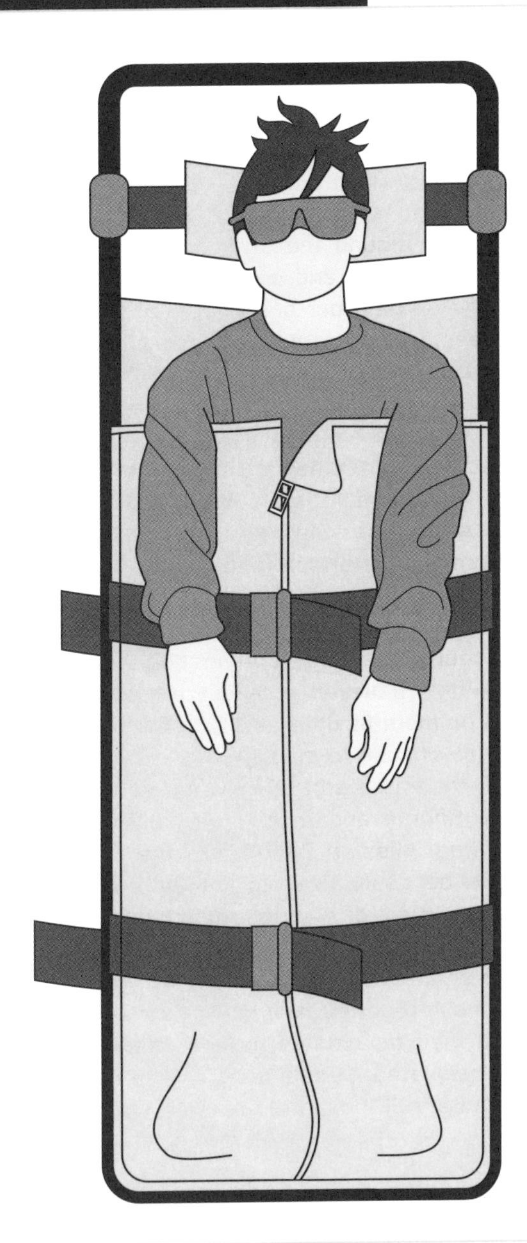

SLEEPING QUARTERS FEATURE COMFORTABLE RESTRAINTS THAT ALLOW FOR A RESTFUL SLEEP.

Crewmembers will provide an eye mask to help you block out ambient light. Your sleeping quarters will vary, depending on your spacecraft. On the Space Shuttle and other station supply craft, you will probably use a special sleeping bag that anchors to a wall; without this attachment, you would float freely around the ship and bump into things, causing you to wake up and possibly injure yourself. The Space Shuttle also has four bunk beds (with tether straps for holding sleeping astronauts in place), but depending on the number of crewmembers on the mission, these might all be occupied at any given time. Astronauts also sleep in the commander's seat or the pilot's seat.

On the Space Station, sleeping is slightly more comfortable. There are two small crew cabins, both of which contain a small sleep "capsule" that affords some privacy. Within each capsule are straps to hold you in place, a small window, a reading light, and a ventilation fan that can be adjusted to regulate airflow.

Most astronauts sleep about eight hours at the end of each mission day. However, as a space tourist, your sleep schedule will be more flexible, and you will be permitted to take naps if you choose to do so.

Fortunately, there is a sort of wake-up service. Mornings on the Space Shuttle and Soyuz, you will awaken to an "alarm" sent from Mission Control; on the Space Shuttle, this alarm can be customized to the astronaut's liking (a favorite piece of music or a song requested by a loved one, for instance). On the International Space Station, you will be awakened by an alarm clock.

Astronauts have reported having dreams and nightmares in space, and their crewmates have occasionally reported snoring. Once adjusted, people generally sleep far better in space than on Earth. Pleasant dreams!

HOW TO SPACEWALK

It's space tourism's ultimate walk on the wild side—the outer-space equivalent of bungee-jumping, parasailing, and skydiving all rolled into one amazing rush. And it's just a single step outside your door.

When you step outside your spacecraft and into space, you leave behind the craft's supplies of air and water, its protection against vacuum and temperature extremes, its shielding against solar radiation, and its seats and handholds for moving around. During a spacewalk, a special Extravehicular Activity (EVA) spacesuit is used to provide these lifelines for a period of several hours.

Without such protection, exposure to the vacuum of space causes quick incapacity and death: The body's internal pressure pushes air and fluids out of all orifices, and a lack of oxygen causes the brain to begin shutting down. Soft tissue begins to swell, and as pressure drops in blood vessels and flesh, dissolved gas froths violently to the surface. Meanwhile, exposed skin undergoes rapid "sunburn" from the unshielded ultraviolet rays of the Sun.

Your EVA spacesuit is designed to provide the same protections and services as a spacecraft, though for shorter periods of time. Several layers of material hold the air in, and outer layers provide insulation and some protection from micrometeorites. A special, highly tinted visor allows you to see your surroundings while blocking ultraviolet rays.

Your life support equipment is stored in a big backpack that weighs almost as much as you do. The backpack contains oxygen bottles, "scrubbers" to clean carbon dioxide from the air you expel, a cooling system that circulates cold water through plastic webbing that surrounds your body, and electrical power for lighting, radio, fans, and other critical systems. Though in microgravity the spacesuit does not have measurable weight, it still has volume and mass, which make all movement in the spacesuit slow and deliberate.

SPACE TRAVELERS DON A SPECIAL EXTRAVEHICULAR ACTIVITY SUIT FOR "WALKING" IN SPACE.

The air pressure inside your spacesuit is lower than Earth's surface pressure, but it is still high enough to expand the suit to a nearly rigid tightness that makes bending an arm or leg difficult. To get an idea of how difficult, imagine trying to deform a fully inflated inner tube. Movement of appendages relies on a system of complex hinge and pulley mechanisms that allows joints to bend (or the hips and wrists to swivel) by keeping the suit's volume as constant as possible. Gloves are generally considered the most difficult part of the suit to master, and hands and fingers get tired quickly without previous strength training.

Because spacewalks last only a few hours, activities like eating and bodily functions are abbreviated. Inside the helmet, there is a water hose to suck on and perhaps a small nutritional bar to eat. The suit includes a flexible tube that allows urination and a "diaper" for accidents. The supreme exertion of a spacewalk will make you sweat constantly: The air purification filters and ventilation systems do their best to reduce overheating and associated odors.

Spacewalk preparation includes an intense period of decompression to avoid "the bends," a dangerous condition that results from the formation of nitrogen bubbles in blood or tissue. Decompression prior to the spacewalk includes a 10-minute period of intense exercise while breathing pure oxygen through a mask. After 50 minutes, the pressure in the spacecraft's airlock is lowered to 10.2 pounds per square inch (70.3 kilopascals), and another 30-minute period of pure oxygen follows. Once in your spacesuit in the airlock, you will breathe pure oxygen for an additional 60 minutes before venturing out of the airlock and into space. Upon your return, you will undergo a similar period of repressurization.

THE SPACE LIFESTYLE

Life in space moves at a different pace from life on Earth. Because of your rapid velocity, days and nights are just 45 minutes long, which can disrupt the body's circadian rhythms. Instead of packing all your activities into daylight hours, tasks are completed during your waking hours, which will include both light and dark periods. Of course, there are still times set aside for meals, bathing, taking pictures, sending e-mail, and talking on the "Softphone." However, in space, many of these tasks are a bit more complicated than on Earth. The following sections describe the key points to help you master space-based activities.

SPACE FOOD AND DRINK: WHAT TO EXPECT

For the modern space traveler, food storage and preparation technologies have advanced far beyond the early days of powdered-everything and Tang. You will have hundreds of meal choices, from pumpkin pie and pork chops to pizza and pretzels. In addition, thanks to frequent resupply missions, visitors to the International Space Station even have access to fresh fruits and vegetables.

There are, however, some important points to understand when preparing for meals in orbit.

TRY BEFORE YOU FLY. Every space traveler must sample space foods on Earth before eating them in orbit, to avoid allergic reactions. You will order your space meals months before your mission actually begins.

BE CAREFUL. In orbit, your spacecraft and all of its contents are in a state of perpetual free fall. In microgravity, anything not secured moves around continuously, and a handful of snacks will float through the air when released. Space food is specially packaged to contain its contents, and not just to make eating easier. Crumbs can kill if inhaled while sleeping in orbit, and the same goes for liquids. Open packages and consume their contents carefully, making sure to quickly grab any items that are released inadvertently.

PREPARE FOR NEW FORMS. Your food will come in one of eight forms: fresh (produce), frozen (chicken pot pie), natural (nuts), irradiated (beef steak), refrigerated (sour cream), thermostabilized (tuna fish), rehydratable (oatmeal), and intermediate moisture (dried apricots, beef jerky). For variety, most meals combine items from several categories. Salt and pepper are available, but only in liquid form, since granular condiments can escape and clog air vents or cause other damage.

EATING AND DRINKING

Before beginning a meal, you will attach a metal meal tray (your "dinner plate") to your lap with a strap; the tray can also be attached to a wall if this is more comfortable. Depending on the food, you may use a pair of scissors to cut open packets before heating or reconstituting your meal. Food is reconstituted by adding hot water or heating in a convection oven.

>> FROM MISSION CONTROL

Microgravity makes otherwise stable eating utensils extremely dangerous. Make sure to stick your magnetic utensils to your tray when they are not in use.

While chewing with

your mouth open is considered rude on Earth, in space it can make a mess. If a clump of food escapes while you are eating, simply bat it back into your mouth using your spoon. It is considered poor orbital etiquette to use food or utensils as weapons (see tip from Mission Control, opposite).

EATING IN SPACE CAN BE COMPLICATED.

"SPACE STRAWS" MINIMIZE MESSY SPILLS.

Drinking in space is not difficult but does require an extra step. You will use a special straw with a clamp on the end. When you are not drinking, make sure the clamp is closed to prevent liquids from leaking out and making a mess.

YOUR WATER SUPPLY

Because water is critical for human life, spacecraft and space stations must keep adequate daily supplies on hand, as well as stocks for emergencies. But the weight and volume displacement of water make it extremely expensive to send into orbit. Although supply ships do bring fresh water to orbit, the International Space Station will eventually rely on two additional methods to create safe drinking water: recycling and condensation collection.

A new recycling system is set to be introduced on the Space Station that will reuse most of the wastewater currently discarded. Under the Water Recycling System (WRS), wastewater (including human and animal urine and so-called gray water, or runoff from bathing and cleaning) is sent through a special system of three filters. The filters remove particles and debris, organic and inorganic compounds, and, finally, bacteria and viruses. The resulting water is cleaner and more pure than the water that comes out of taps on Earth.

Currently, a Russian-built water processor in orbit removes humidity from the air and makes the collected water suitable for drinking. However, because some water is always lost during recycling, fresh water will continue to be delivered via supply ships for the foreseeable future.

BATHING IN SPACE

Microgravity makes traditional showers or baths impossible in outer space. However, you are encouraged to bathe once per day. To do so, you will take a "sponge bath," using one washcloth for cleaning and one for rinsing. (To conserve water, washcloths are moistened using spray bottles instead of water from a tap.) In some settings, you may use moistened "baby wipes" instead of washcloths. Rinseless shampoo will be provided for your hair.

Soap and water stick to the skin in microgravity, so you will "dry and rinse" using a vacuum system that sucks excess water off the body and stores it in a wastewater tank. Toothpaste can be swallowed or sucked out in a fashion similar to the suction tube used by dentists.

Though there is no beauty salon on the Space Station, you can get a haircut, should you be away from Earth for long periods. Hair is cut using standard shears; it then floats freely. The cut hair is sucked from the cabin with a hose and vacuum collector and moved to a storage tank for disposal later. Due to microgravity, it is impossible to apply nail polish in space, so manicures are not among the present offerings.

USING THE TOILET

In the zero-gravity, tightly controlled life support environment in spacecraft and aboard space stations, there are no traditional "bathrooms." Instead, waste collection and disposal devices generally take one of two forms.

BODY ATTACHED COLLECTORS

During launch, reentry, spacewalks, and any time you are not on a space station or shuttle, you will urinate and/or defecate into what is, essentially, an adult diaper. Although some of these collectors have hoses that conveniently hook up to the appropriate body part, the process is not especially enjoyable and it can be laborious to self-cleanse afterward (particularly with regard to expelling solid waste).

You should generally avoid defecation until you have access to a vacuum collector. Before launch, you will fast for several hours prior to liftoff and obtain a preflight enema.

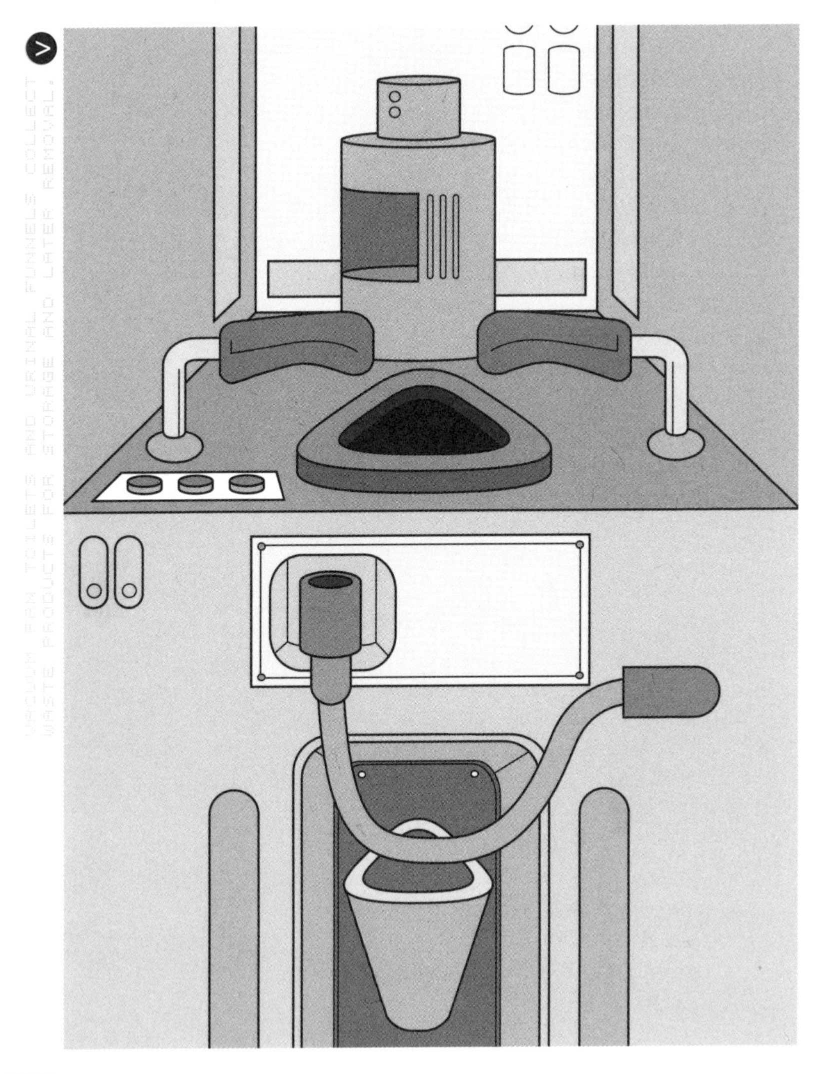

> VACUUM FAN TOILETS AND URINAL FUNNELS COLLECT WASTE PRODUCTS FOR STORAGE AND LATER REMOVAL.

VACUUM COLLECTORS

Onboard the ISS, other space stations, and the Space Shuttle, waste disposal is, if not enjoyable, more pleasant. A vacuum fan toilet collects and sends waste for storage and later removal. Both women and men can stand to urinate if they choose, but both must sit on the vacuum toilet to defecate. When using vacuum collectors, follow these general guidelines.

01: **GET COMFORTABLE.** When sitting on the vacuum toilet, make sure there is a tight seal between your body and the toilet seat: Use the thigh bars and attached leg and foot restraints to stay in position. Remember, any gap may allow waste to float out of the toilet and into the cabin.

02: **ATTACH THE URINAL FUNNEL.** Each space traveler is issued a personal urinal funnel that attaches to the urinal hose's adapter. Make sure your funnel is secure before proceeding. If standing, secure feet using foot restraints. It is considered rude to use another astronaut's funnel; if you've lost yours, ask a crewmember to provide a new one.

03: **AIM CAREFULLY.** Though the vacuum collector is powerful, it will not suck down everything floating in the vicinity. Make sure your waste is released close enough to the hose collector or vacuum toilet to be taken in by the suction. Neither the hose nor the toilet requires flushing.

04: **CLEAN UP.** Your solid waste will be dehydrated for more efficient storage. You now have only one task left to perform: As a courtesy to your crewmates, be sure to clean the area with one of the disposable sanitary cloths stored next to the vacuum toilet.

SPACE SUNSCREEN: SKIN AND EYE PRECAUTIONS

During launch and return from orbit, you will don a spacesuit and a helmet with a protective visor that shields you from harmful radiation. Once in orbit, however, you will be in a "shirtsleeve" environment and will rely on sunscreen and your spacecraft to shield you from solar radiation and cosmic rays.

Solar radiation is stronger in space than on Earth, because you will not have the planet's atmosphere to protect you. You should bring and wear the highest-rated sunscreen you can find to reduce the chance of "solar burn." Pay special attention to your face, which can burn quickly just from looking out the windows of the Space Station. Always make sure to wear sunglasses with full UV protection when looking out the windows and, as on Earth, never, ever look directly at the Sun, or you risk burning your cornea.

RADIATION PROTECTION

Even on Earth, we are exposed to background radiation all the time. For an extended stay in space (six months), you can expect to receive about 80 milliSieverts (mSv) of radiation; 1 mSv of space radiation is approximately equal to receiving three chest X-rays. Your visit, however, is likely to be significantly shorter than six months, with a resultant lower dose of radiation: about .5 mSv per day, or 4 to 5 mSv for a one-week stay.

While on board, however, you will wear a small dosimeter, a device that measures the amount of radiation you are exposed to. Dosimeters built into the station itself also constantly monitor the safety of the interior environment and give warnings if levels of radiation become abnormally high.

In general, the areas where you and your crewmembers spend the most time (crew quarters, galley) are heavily shielded, often with materials such as polyethylene, which has a high hydrogen content; such materials have been shown to offer more protection from radiation than metals.

Altitude and orbit inclination also play a role in determining how much radiation spacecraft are exposed to. At higher altitudes, the Earth's magnetic field is weaker, and space travelers are exposed to more solar radiation. Radiation levels are also much higher at the Earth's poles, one reason orbits with a polar inclination have thus far been unmanned.

HOW TO AVOID SPACE SICKNESS

Weightlessness is very confusing to the human brain. Though the eyes tell the brain what is "up" and what is "down" in a spaceship or space station, the vestibular organs in the inner ear—which help maintain balance and rely on the downward pull of gravity to function—do not work properly in microgravity. The brain receives conflicting signals and may respond by causing headache, disorientation, nausea, and loss of appetite.

The sensation of space sickness is similar to air sickness, car sickness, or sea sickness. Your equilibrium is upset, and as a result, you feel awful. Do you know that queasy feeling you get when experiencing a

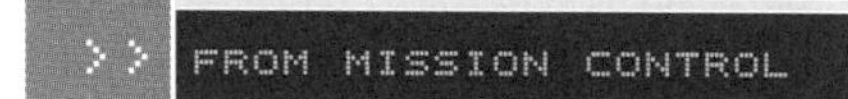

To experience the sensation of space sickness on planet Earth, lie flat and face down on a bed, looking at the floor. Tilt your head downward, over the edge of the bed, about five degrees from horizontal. This tilt reproduces the shift of body fluids encountered in microgravity. Or try a headstand, which similarly upsets your equilibrium.

steep drop on a roller coaster? In space, this feeling can persist for hours or even days.

People have different tolerances and thresholds for space sickness, but even the toughest body will fall prey to motion sickness under severe circumstances. The good news is that the brain adapts to the situation after some time, and the balance system eventually gets back on track.

Thankfully, there are ways to ease the quease:

- Change your position slowly, and avoid sudden side-to-side head movements.
- Focus on fixed points when you are still.
- Look straight ahead rather than at your feet.
- Use motion-sickness medication, including a Scopolamine patch, Scope-Dex (a mixture of Scopolamine and Dexedrine), or oral Phenagren (NASA has found that it significantly reduces the incidence of motion sickness).

REMEMBER: Everything floats in microgravity, and space sickness can be very messy if you are not well prepared. Keep a sickness bag on hand at all times if you feel ill.

EXERCISING IN SPACE

Before signing up for space flight, you may not have had a daily workout regimen on Earth. In orbit, however, exercise is mandatory, and with good reason. In space, you will suffer bone and muscle deterioration over time, because the body does not encounter the resistance that is generated by gravity.

The physiological changes that occur in space flight are similar to those seen with extended bed rest: Muscles lose strength and mass, bones and tendons shrink and weaken, and once-simple tasks become difficult or impossible. Skipping exercise during an extended stay in space means you may not be able to walk properly when you return to Earth.

To counteract the adverse effects of weightlessness, especially on the back and leg muscles that help you stand up on Earth, flight doctors require 15 minutes of strenuous exercise daily on 7- to 14-day missions and 30 minutes of exercise daily on month-long missions. Because even the easiest exercise on Earth (walking, for example) relies on the resistance generated by gravity, exercise in space is slightly more complicated, though not uncomfortably so.

Thankfully, most space destinations will feature state-of-the-art fitness facilities to help you accomplish your tasks. As you work out, moving air from a nearby duct helps dry perspiration (without this air supply, sweat would stick unpleasantly to your skin instead of dripping off as it does on Earth). Your outer space fitness facility may include any of the following machines:

- CYCLE ERGOMETER: The ISS has a special cycling machine called the cycle ergometer that exercises the heart and legs and is also used to measure vital signs. The main activity is pedaling, as on a stationary bicycle.

- TREADMILL: The treadmill is a Teflon-coated aluminum sheet on a roller, with a bottom that locks into holes in the floor. Harnesses from the base of the treadmill attach to your body so you won't float away. Users can exercise their arms by pushing upward on the bar while walking or jogging.

SPACE TREADMILLS FEATURE SPECIAL RESTRAINTS THAT ALLOW YOU TO JOG IN ZERO-GRAVITY CONDITIONS.

RESISTANCE EXERCISE DEVICE (RED): The RED is a machine similar to a Soloflex that uses a system of rubber cords and pulleys to create resistance. The RED is a versatile piece of equipment that can be used for a variety of exercises, including squats, arm curls, knee bends, leg lifts, and heel raises.

07: THE VOYAGE HOME

All good vacations must come to an end. Fortunately, a return trip to Earth is much shorter than a launch to outer space. In this chapter, we'll review the best ways to ensure a safe trip home, with all of your souvenirs and appendages intact.

PREPARING FOR EARTH RETURN

As with any conventional vacation, you'll need to prepare before returning home. It's time to gather your belongings, discard your trash, and pack up. But in space, you can't just toss garbage bags into a Dumpster and throw your clothes into the trunk of the car—again, a bit more planning and effort is required.

SPACE GARBAGE

On the Space Station, you have two options for garbage disposal: Ship it back to Earth, or incinerate it. The station's solid waste, especially used food packages, empty fuel containers, and refuse from scientific experiments, cannot simply be ejected into space: The debris could damage satellites or cause problems for other spacecraft in orbit or for the Space Station itself.

If your crew is shipping garbage back to Earth, trash will be placed in sealed containers, transferred to the ship's cargo bay, and brought back to Earth to be recycled or disposed of by conventional methods.

Incineration is another solution. Unmanned and disposable supply ships can serve as an incinerator for any trash placed aboard. Refuse should be packed in large garbage bags, which are transferred to the ship while it is still connected to the Space Station. When the ship is full, it is sealed, detached from the station, and sent into a lower orbit. From there, the ship deorbits at a speed and declination that cause it to burn up upon entering Earth's atmosphere. The ship enters the atmosphere over the ocean, in case any dangerous particles remain after incineration.

WHERE TO STOW EXTRA STUFF ON BOARD

Before leaving the Space Station and returning to Earth, you will be required to gather all of your personal belongings and stow them in the descent module. Take the following steps before the capsule undocks from the Space Station.

REVIEW PERSONAL ITEMS CHECKLIST. Closely review the checklist on page 124 and make certain you have each and every item you brought with you. You will not be able to "turn around" once you undock, and anything left behind isn't likely to come back to Earth until the next manned supply mission, if at all.

USE BULKHEAD POUCHES. There will be small storage pouches on the bulkheads of the descent module. Use these for small items such as souvenirs and "space gifts" (see the chart on page 123 for items that can serve as space gifts).

USE SPACE UNDER SEAT. There is a small storage compartment under your seat which can be used for a laptop computer and other small electronic devices.

USE WALL-MOUNTED COMPARTMENTS. Small storage compartments built into the interior of the reentry capsule will accommodate any remaining personal items.

DOUBLE-CHECK. Make certain all items are securely stored and compartment doors are fully closed. There should be no loose items onboard the descent module.

REENTRY AND LANDING

It all comes down to this—literally. Time your reentry correctly, and you'll have survived the greatest vacation available to humankind. But we're warning you now: The ride won't be a smooth one.

PREPARING FOR REENTRY

You will experience higher Gs and more discomfort on reentry than you did on launch. Fortunately, the deorbit and reentry processes take just a few hours, with only a few minutes of high G-loads.

01: USE THE BATHROOM BEFORE YOU UNDOCK. There are no "facilities" in the reentry module, just your "adult diaper." Use the vacuum toilet just before you strap yourself into the Soyuz.

02: DON YOUR MEDICAL HARNESS. Carefully pull on your medical harness, which Mission Control will use to monitor your vital signs during reentry. Make sure there is tight contact between the sensors and your skin to ensure accuracy.

03: EXAMINE YOUR SPACESUIT FOR HOLES OR TEARS. If you notice a potential hazard, alert a member of the crew and ask for assistance. Otherwise, proceed to put on the spacesuit.

04: TAKE YOUR SEAT. You should be fully strapped into your personal seat liner and seat in the reentry module. Your body may have lengthened slightly during your trip, so be sure to adjust belts accordingly. (In the microgravity of space, the vertebrae of the spine are not as compressed as they are on Earth, giving space travelers slightly more height. You will shrink to your preflight height after returning to your home planet.) Snap your visor into the down position.

05: CHECK COMMUNICATIONS GEAR. Talk to Mission Control, and make sure you can hear any instructions. The flight cabin and crew will soon be ready for departure.

HOW TO BREATHE AT 7 GS

On reentry, the G-forces in the descent module will be at the highest of any point during your trip. Forces may be as high as 7 Gs for a few seconds at maximum acceleration, with lower levels (about 3 Gs) for stretches of a few minutes. Use the tips below to make the G-forces more manageable.

01: BREATHE IN LARGE GULPS. With the extreme pressure on your body, you will find getting air into your lungs labored. Pushing out with your stomach muscles, expand your abdomen and then suck it in quickly, taking in large gulps of air.

02: KEEP YOUR STOMACH, ARM, AND LEG MUSCLES TENSE TO COUNTER THE PRESSURE. Don't relax your abdomen, or breathing will be nearly impossible.

03: KEEP YOUR HEAD BACK AGAINST YOUR SEAT LINER. You will be in the fetal position, with your back toward Earth. If you move your head forward, you risk having it pushed to the side in an uncomfortable position, pinching a nerve, and getting stuck in this position until the Gs diminish.

04: BEGIN TO TAKE MORE BREATHS. As your altitude and acceleration decrease, Gs will begin to fall. At about 3 Gs, breathing will be less strained but still difficult. Take shorter breaths instead of big gulps of air.

LANDING

For space travelers, returning to Earth on the Soyuz spacecraft will be an exhilarating yet potentially frightening experience. The G-forces, the flames outside the windows, and the creaking of the spacecraft's exterior all make deorbit and reentry something you will never forget.

After the pilot has undocked the Soyuz capsule and backed it away from the Space Station, he will order the rocket firing that sends the spaceship out of its orbit and into the upper atmosphere.

Approximately half an hour after the rocket firing, you will notice floating dust particles begin to sink to the floor of the spacecraft: This is the first indication of atmosphere reentry and the beginning of G-load effect as your spaceship encounters progressively thicker layers of air. From this point forward, G-forces increase rapidly, and you must be prepared.

01: KEEP YOUR BODY LOOSE, AND TAKE DEEP, MEASURED BREATHS. You will feel the direct sensation of G-load pressure on your body, often referred to as a "burden on the body." This sensation will be accompanied by labored breathing and speech. These conditions are all part of the reentry experience and are normal.

02: DO NOT SWALLOW OR TALK. You will begin to experience the sensation of a lump in your throat as the intense G-forces press down on your Adam's apple and esophagus. Try not to swallow or talk during this period, as both will be difficult.

03: **WATCH FOR WARNING SIGNS.** Several minutes into reentry, check your vision for an indicator of possibly serious effects of the G-forces. Look for tunnel vision or "red-out," a red haze moving across your field of vision. If you begin to experience either symptom, prepare to counteract the effects of high-G. To force blood back to your head, create additional body tension: Increase abdominal pressure by sucking your gut in, and flex your leg muscles. If problems persist, inflate the air cuffs around your legs.

04: **REMEMBER YOUR TRAINING.** As you approach the lower atmosphere, the G-forces will begin to drop off—the sensation will be similar to the slowing of the centrifuge during your training. Tighten your restraint system, especially at your hips and legs.

05: **PREPARE FOR PARACHUTE DEPLOYMENT.** At a preset speed and altitude, the capsule's drogue and primary parachutes will deploy. You will experience a sudden deceleration, often described as a strong tugging or yanking feeling. These feelings are normal and may be accompanied by temporary dizziness. Just after deployment, the capsule hangs at an angle (to maximize air flow cooling across the heat shield), then pops to a straight up-down alignment.

06: **TAKE STEPS TO COMBAT MOTION SICKNESS.** As it floats to Earth under its parachutes, the Soyuz capsule may spin quickly on the shroud lines; this is normal. The spinning, however, may induce or aggravate vestibular (middle ear) irritations and cause motion sickness. Many different sensations are possible: vertigo, postural illusions, general discomfort, and nausea. To combat these feelings, limit head and eye movement and fix your gaze on a motionless object; the instrument panel works well.

07: **POSITION YOUR BODY FOR LANDING.** Your landing will be softened by the timed firing of six small rocket engines at the base of the capsule; these are exposed when the heat shield is jettisoned. Your seat is elevated so its supports flex on contact with the ground. As a result, make sure your arms are properly in their restraints to avoid twisting of arms or wrists when the capsule touches down.

08: **MOVE SLOWLY.** Welcome back to Earth. Do not get up too quickly: Stay in your chair for several minutes, then stand up slowly. Upon standing, limit your head and eye movement, and avoid any excessive motion. Proceed slowly and do not confront the Earth's gravity in an upright position too quickly.

WHAT TO DO IF THE CAPSULE DEPRESSURIZES

Although rare, depressurization of the descent module (due to a leaky valve or other system failure) can cause complications. Should you experience a sudden depressurization during deorbit and reentry, take the following steps.

01: **STAY CALM.** Your Sokol spacesuit is fully pressurized and is designed to protect you in the event of a depressurization emergency.

02: **LIMIT MOVEMENT.** Moving will be very difficult if there is a loss of capsule pressure, and activity will be further impeded by the high Gs. Keep your head back against your seat to prevent strains or pinched nerves in your neck.

03: **PREPARE FOR CHILL.** Loss of pressure will make the cabin extremely cold.

04: **CHECK PRESSURE GAUGE.** When the descent module reaches about 10,000 feet (3.05 km), it will begin to repressurize automatically; valves adjust the internal pressure so the capsule door can be opened once you are on the ground. Check the gauge on the arm of your spacesuit to get a pressure reading.

05: **MOVE SLOWLY.** Once you are on the ground, make careful, measured movements as the cabin repressurizes.

HOW TO SURVIVE A WATER LANDING

The descent module on the Soyuz is designed for landing on the ground. However, there are contingencies and equipment in place for a water landing, should the capsule go off course during reentry, or should an aborted launch cause the escape rocket to send the capsule over water.

01: **STAY CALM.** The descent module is watertight and buoyant. It has sufficient air for three people to breath for 15 hours. After this period, vents to the outside can be opened to let in ambient air.

02: **DETERMINE POSITION.** You will feel the capsule bobbing and floating in the water. Look out one of the capsule windows (on the port and starboard sides) to determine the module's orientation. The hatch on the module is on the top and should be facing up and be clear of water.

03: **PREPARE OTHER SUPPLIES.** The descent module contains emergency survival equipment, including life

IN THE EVENT OF A WATER
LANDING, MISSION CONTROL WILL
SEND SHIPS AND HELICOPTERS TO
THE TOUCHDOWN SITE.

jackets, personal rafts, pullovers, exposure suits, radios, and emergency flares.

04: **RADIO FOR HELP.** In the unlikely event of a water landing, Mission Control will send ships and helicopters to the touchdown area to rescue the crew and recover the capsule. If you cannot communicate with Mission Control using the capsule's communication systems, turn your portable radio on, tune it to VHF 121.5, and wait for instructions.

05: **WAIT FOR RESCUE.** Rescuers will first secure the capsule to the side of a ship (or lift it via crane or helicopter) before opening the hatch; failure to do so could result in the tipping of the capsule and water entering through the hatch. (In 1961, the *Liberty Bell 7* capsule, with astronaut Gus Grissom aboard, began to sink after a hatch on the module was blown prematurely. Grissom survived but was killed six years later in the *Apollo 1* fire.) The capsule should be attached to a ship using steel cables hooked to the parachute harness system on the side of the module. Once the hatch has been opened, climb out. If no rescuers arrive, continue to Step 6.

06: **EVACUATE.** Put on your life jacket and wet suit. Open the hatch. Holding your supply kit and life raft, climb out of the capsule and into the water. Inflate your raft and climb in. Do not attempt to inflate your raft while still inside the capsule. Continue to radio for help until rescuers arrive.

GETTING USED TO GRAVITY (AGAIN)

Upon your return to Earth, it is critical that you allow your bones, muscles, and vestibular system to readjust to normal gravity. Use the tips below as a guide to proper reacclimation.

01: **EXPECT LIGHTHEADEDNESS.** You may experience sudden nausea, dizzy spells, and lightheadedness as the organs and nerves in your inner ear readjust to gravity. These symptoms should pass in a few days. In the meantime, avoid fast head movement, and avoid cycling, skating, gymnastics, or other sports that require continuous balance.

02: **MOVE SLOWLY.** Your body moves much faster on Earth than in the microgravity of space. Actions like grabbing objects with your hands and moving your legs will take fractions of a second, instead of several seconds. Move slowly at first, until your brain "remembers" how much effort particular actions require.

03: **DO NOT STRAIN MUSCLES AND BONES.** Avoid immediate exercise, and use caution when lifting heavy objects. You may have lost some muscle mass and bone density, especially if you've been in orbit for several weeks. (NASA research has shown that Space Station astronauts, on average, lose interior bone density at a rate of 2.2 to 2.7 percent per month and outer bone density at a rate of 1.6 to 1.7 percent per month.) Ease into physical activity to avoid possible fractures.

04: **GRADUALLY INCREASE ACTIVITY LEVELS.** Several days after your return, begin to increase your physical activity level. Start with long walks, then advance to jogging and more strenuous exercise. You will need moderate levels of activity to strengthen stability muscles, which protect bones and joints.

08: WHAT'S NEXT?

Nearly every opportunity described within these pages is available to would-be space tourists right now. If you're interested in signing up or want to know about potential future developments for the space tourism industry, read on.

LEARNING MORE

Space tourism, once the province of science fiction, is now a reality. There are a lot of resources on the World Wide Web that can help you learn more about space flight and the important new developments now taking place in commercial space travel.

SPACEFLIGHT.NASA.GOV is an excellent repository of information about the United States space program, the International Space Station, and the history of space exploration.

WWW.SPACE.COM covers both existing space missions and the technological breakthroughs that are critical to private space travel.

WWW.EDLU.COM is the site of U.S. astronaut Ed Lu and contains the journals written during his six-month stay on the International Space Station.

WWW.XPRIZE.ORG is an excellent site to learn about the new space vehicles that competed for the $10-million ANSARI X Prize. On October 4, 2004, the X Prize was awarded to the owners of *SpaceShipOne*, the first private spacecraft to reach 62 miles (100 km) altitude, return safely to Earth, and repeat the same trip within two weeks.

WWW.VIRGINGALACTIC.COM details Sir Richard Branson's plans for commercial space flight on *SpaceShipOne*-based craft.

WWW.SPACEADVENTURES.COM provides in-depth information on the programs available today for space tourists, including space flights, astronaut training, and other space flight–simulation experiences.

One of the best ways to learn more about the exciting developments in commercial space flight is to join Space Adventures' Spaceflight Club. Even if you're not ready to spend millions on a trip to the International Space Station, membership in the Spaceflight Club gives you access to special VIP events, new technology demos, an annual conference, and newsletters with the most recent developments in private space flight. Best of all, membership dues will be applied to your first sub-orbital space flight. For more information, see page 192.

A TRIP OF A LIFETIME, AND A TRIP FOR HUMANKIND

A trip to space is the ultimate vacation, and your journey will stay with you for the rest of your life. But any flight to orbit is much more than a flight of fancy: Space travel has numerous benefits for humans as a species, from critical scientific experiments to the development of new technologies that can make life on Earth better.

The process of getting to and exploring space has some very practical elements, virtually all of which have direct consequences for life on Earth today. These include the creation of new systems for transportation, new means of energy production, and the capability to develop settlements on other worlds—settlements that may one day provide a refuge from a disaster on Earth.

Space exploration, more than any other pursuit, is intrinsic to developing new and better transportation systems. Such systems would not be used just for space travel. New designs for spacecraft will eventually filter down to commercial aviation systems, while advances in propulsion, materials, and electronics will be used by any number of terrestrial modes of transport, from submarines to cars to trains.

Because of the high speeds and vast distances involved, space travel is also critical to the development of new types of energy, including space-based and beamed solar power. The expense and complexity of carrying cargo to orbit demand lighter, more efficient, and more renewable sources of fuel that will eventually allow humans to visit other planets that are too far for current technologies. As new energy sources for space travel are developed and perfected, they will make their way back to Earth in the form of new power-generation facilities that are many times more efficient than today's models.

The long-term viability of the human race is dependent upon space travel. For the species to survive a catastrophic Earth calamity (whether natural or man-made), we must find a way to survive and reproduce beyond our own planet. Whether this will be on ships or space stations or other planets is unknown at this point. But few would argue with the premise that the only reliable way to ensure our survival is to create a livable space environment not subject to nuclear destruction, deadly climate change, or the massive annihilation that would result from an asteroid impact. Without an eventual space settlement, we put our future at grave risk.

FUTURE PLANS

We are lucky enough to be living at the most exciting time in the history of private space travel. While Space Adventures has already sent the first few tourists into orbit, we are on the cusp of new technologies that will make commercial space flight faster, easier, and more affordable than ever before.

New space vehicles have already completed test flights and will be available for paying customers within the next few years. Private space stations are under development, and prototypes are under construction.

Promising new technologies are currently being investigated as more fuel-efficient ways to send spacecraft into space. In particular, laser propulsion is a promising solution to the limitations of today's conventional chemical propulsion systems.

Current rockets are basically flying fuel towers; conventional rockets' need to store and drag along huge amounts of energy is the major reason that space flight is so expensive. The fuel demands of current rockets also increase the risks of catastrophic failure and reduce payload capacity—the rocket's most important characteristic.

Laser propulsion (also called "beamed-energy propulsion") may be the answer to the problems associated with conventional chemical rockets. A laser-propelled spacecraft (or "lightcraft") would be the size and weight of a midsized car. The lightcraft would be able to take three people safely and comfortably to and from low Earth orbit on one small tank of fuel.

Lightcraft generate thrust by focusing an Earth-based beam of pulsed laser energy to a point behind the vehicle. The air at the focal point is super heated into a plasma pulse that propels the lightcraft through the air. When the lightcraft climbs out of Earth's atmosphere, onboard fuel is used for propellant. The main advantage of laser propulsion is that most of the energy used to propel the vehicle remains on the ground with the laser. Additionally, the most expensive part of the rocket—the engines, or in the case of a lightcraft, the laser—remain safely on the ground to be reused for later flights.

A laser-powered orbital space transportation system would use a giant 1.5-gigawatt laser to propel a three-person vehicle to orbit. Laser propulsion has been demonstrated with model vehicles flying along a laser beam to more than 500 feet (152.4 m).

Other new orbital propulsion systems, including solar sails, space tethers, and even a "space elevator" may eventually be built with the help of private companies and private-sector know-how.

In the end, the only limit to how far humans can travel is the limit of our collective imagination. Technology isn't always equal to the task of building our dreams, of course, and the costs of and technical barriers to commercial space travel are still fairly high. But if the space race of the 1960s—the Golden Decade of space flight—proved anything, it's that human ingenuity can overcome seemingly insurmountable obstacles. With the will, we will find the way.

And, indeed, we must find new ways, and better ways, to send humans into space. After all, we really have no choice. The Earth's resources are finite, and a cataclysmic event is virtually assured at some point in the future. As a species, our future depends on our ability to make it to other worlds. The question is not if we will get there, but when, and how.

MEASUREMENTS

Whenever possible, we have included U.S. and metric measurements throughout this book. If you have additional data that you would like to convert, use this chart to navigate between the two systems.

1 foot	.3 meter
1 meter	3.28 feet
1 kilometer	0.62 mile
1 mile	1.61 kilometer
1 kilogram	2.20 pounds
1 pound	.45 kilograms
0° Celsius	32° Fahrenheit
0° Fahrenheit	-17.78° Celsius
Speed of sound (on Earth)	761.21 miles per hour
Speed of light (in space)	670,616,629.38 miles per hour

INDEX

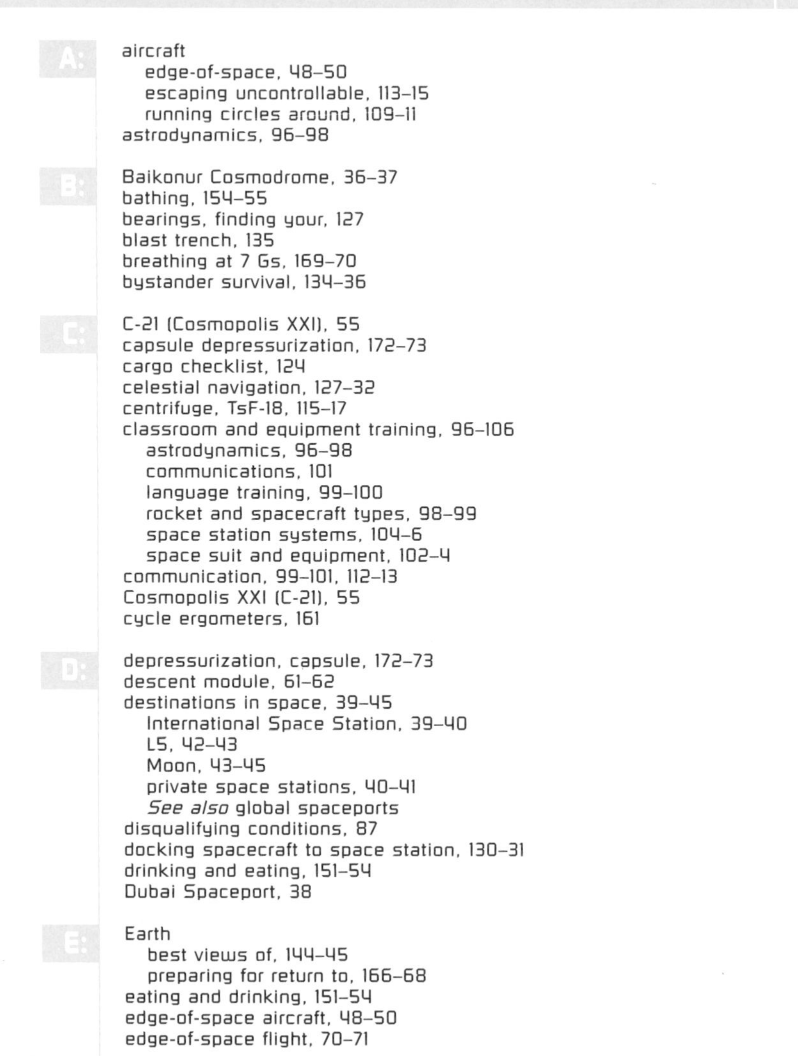